LIVING DEATH
ZOMBIE APOCALYPSE

DAVID MUSSER

Copyright (C) 2023 David Musser

Layout design and Copyright (C) 2023 by Next Chapter

Published 2023 by Next Chapter

Edited by Tom Vater

Cover art by Lordan June Pinote

This book is a work of fiction. Names, characters, places, and incidents are the product of the author's imagination or are used fictitiously. Any resemblance to actual events, locales, or persons, living or dead, is purely coincidental.

All rights reserved. No part of this book may be reproduced or transmitted in any form or by any means, electronic or mechanical, including photocopying, recording, or by any information storage and retrieval system, without the author's permission.

This is my fourth novella, and I am just so happy with the feedback thus far. I dedicate this book to zombie fans. I know that there are many of us. This genre has been such fun for me to read over the years and I just want to give back a little.

ACKNOWLEDGMENTS

You, the Reader – I hope that you'll continue to enjoy my work. Please provide feedback. My plan is to try and continue as long as you are enjoying my stories. KeepInTheLight.com

Megan Anderson – My editor for the **Keep in the Light** series. I would never have started this journey without you believing in me.

Rachel Musser – As always, I am proud of you and could not do what I do without you being just an amazing daughter.

Tom Vater - Thank you for helping to restore my faith in my story telling abilities. A great editor can and did make a wonderful difference to this love story to the Zombie genre.

PREFACE
DOCTORS OFFICE

I'm not sure how I got to this point. Life has a funny way of catching up with you. I've always been told that it is best to start at the beginning to tell a story. Please excuse these recordings. I found one of those old tape machines that lawyers used to use, and I've been recording on it for a while.

Not sure what I was doing, other than capturing the moments. Perhaps a tiny part of me knew that I would end up here.

It really all started about a year ago…

"This is just bullshit," I said as I walked out of the doctor's office. I mean, what the fuck? Who the hell did he think he was? I loved his bedside manner! How hard was it? I'd asked for the results over the phone… I knew I was dying. It was easy to understand the symptoms, and add that to the Internet research I had done, sure enough, I was on the way out.

"You're gonna die!" my search results said.

Well, not exactly, but before I go on, don't feel sorry for me. You know, I'm not a nice person. I just wanted to know for sure

PREFACE

that the Internet was right. To back up a bit. I'd taken the day off a couple of weeks earlier and gone in for many, many tests. The doctor's office called me later on. I never spoke to the doctor, but one of his assistants, a physician's assistant, or some horseshit like that.

"Oh, no, I'm sorry," she'd said, "I don't have access to the results. I'm just calling to set up an appointment for you."

Translation: "I have the results, but we can't bill you unless you come into the office."

"It's our policy," she'd added with just a hint of sadness in her voice.

I showed up at the office fifteen minutes early, the same as I've done for any meeting in my adult life, and I sat, waited, waited, and waited some more. Forty-five fucking minutes later, they told me, "Please go on back."

This time, the nurse, and it was a nurse, not the physician's assistant, took my blood pressure, and frowned because it was elevated. If you kept me in a waiting room for thirty minutes past my appointment, guess what? My blood pressure will go up.

Then the doctor walked in, wearing a golf course tan, holding out his hand for me to shake it. For some reason, I did. I shook it the way my father had taught me, making eye contact.

"Mr. ...," he started, before taking a more personal tone, "Nick, I have bad news."

Well, you can guess where the rest of the conversation went. He talked about types of treatment and dismissed all of the research into alternative medicine I had done.

"Those home treatments never work. Natural remedies don't help."

Blah blah blah. He sounded like the teacher from an old cartoon I had watched as a kid, and I tuned out the rest.

He must have thought I was in shock, because he reached to touch my shoulder to comfort me. Now his nurse, she would have comforted me if she'd wanted a touch, but not this jackass.

To explain, I should say that I was raised in a time when you followed certain protocols when talking to people. You would stand when a lady entered the room, you would shake hands standing, and you never called anyone by their first name without permission. It just wasn't done, but now that I was fucking dying, he thought he could call me Nick.

Okay, thinking back on it I know that I was using that as a reason to be pissed off at something other than the fact that I was dying. I get that. I really do, but you must understand this is the first time I've tried to tell this story. I've been too busy living it. This is the first time that I've had something interesting to tell, and I may not have a lot of time so please forgive me and let me figure out how to get the words out.

Now, where was I? Yes, that was it, I stormed out of the doctor's office, mad for no real reason but mad. I was looking for a reason to go off. I was looking to focus my anger on anything except what I was really angry about.

Did I tell the doctor off before I left? You bet I did. He started to do what they all do and left the paper on the table, saying the nurse would be back in, and I could pay up front and schedule my next visit.

"Cha-ching", he must have thought he was going to have me and my insurance company on the hook for… well, at least a year, maybe a little longer, if I followed his protocols.

When he laid the paper down, I pulled out my money clip. Yes, I am that type of person. I laid five hundred-dollar bills on the paper and said, "Consider my account paid up; send any overpayment please to the local food bank."

And I left the room smiling.

The nurse didn't smile on the way down the hall. She had already been notified to go into my room and when we passed, she was confused. I winked at her and knew she secretly wanted me.

Here I was outside, feeling pissed… Yes, yes, I know for no reason. But I was pissed and was looking for an excuse. The doctor's office was in a little strip mall just on the edge of town. Apart from the doctor's office, there was a grocery store chain, the ABC store.

"What's an ABC store?" you ask.

Well, in order to keep alcohol properly regulated, and not allow local people to make money on it, some states ran ABC stores. Kinda odd when you figure that a lot of state money was spent on police trying to find people driving after drinking too much.

Back to where I was. Sorry I'm dyslexic and my mind wanders, and sometimes being left-handed, I feel I'm not in my right mind. Tell me you got that joke… please?

Okay back to where I was. I was walking to my car, and I saw some other jackass. There are a lot of jackasses in my town. I saw some jackass smack his girlfriend.

He was standing right out in the open, "Don't you backtalk me, Jenny," I heard and then I saw his hand pull back, and smack.

I looked around. All other people in the vicinity were trying to look anywhere except at them. One person was so engrossed in his phone a bomb could have gone off and he would not have noticed. Now to make it even better… They were parked right next to my car.

Her boyfriend was called Todd. I found this out later. His new convertible had its white top up, and the car was baby blue, with a black stripe down the front. This jackass didn't deserve such a beautiful car or the girl.

Me, I was in a POS, a little-known car. Most of the label had worn off, and it was covered in rust. Everyone called this four-door monstrosity by its given name.

"Whose piece of shit is parked in the fire lane?"

I'm sure that I've heard that a dozen times over the years.

The brakes were bad, some would say non-existent, and it was a lot easier to park in the fire lane and let it coast to a stop when I had to run into the ABC store, or collect a pizza at the local pub that sold beer to go.

Jenny turned defiantly and said, "Hit me again, Todd and I'll go home with…"

Then she caught my eye. Seeing as I was the only one around not only watching, but headed in her direction. I guess it wasn't hard. He was twenty-one perhaps, and I guessed she was the same age.

"Him, I'll go home with him and fuck his brains out."

And as God was my witness, she winked at me. It was such a playful wink, and it came with a smile that almost stopped me in my tracks. But I was still mad from the doctor's visit. I had found someone I could hit and take my misery out on. I kept moving forward.

He started to pull back his arm for another smack, and I saw him close his hand into a fist. This one was going to be a punch.

"Throw that punch, junior, and I'll beat you half to death, and take your car and your girl," I said, while I tried to keep my voice calm and hid the joy I felt listening to my own words.

This was gonna be fun, I thought. It had been a long time since I got to cut loose. I'm a widower and when my wife Pam died, I spent many nights in bars, challenging anyone to fight. I found that these days, people were more likely to call their lawyer than return a punch. It was kind of sad.

I trained a little in a martial arts dojo in Front Royal, VA, but I'd run short of time and didn't stick with it. I had the skills I'd learned and then some, so I did some bouncing after I'd left school and that was where I'd met Pam.

She had been on a date that had gotten too handsy on the dance floor, and next thing you know, I threw him out and we got married. We lasted twenty years. We didn't have kids. We thought of adopting, but never got around to it. We both worked a lot, and we did travel a little, but we never got to take the big trips. We were going to sell everything and get one of those big RVs to tour the country. Fate had other plans.

PREFACE

It was a quick death, at least for her. An ice storm a couple of years ago, a deer on the road. Instead of just plastering it across the windshield, she tried to swerve around it. The car behind her stopped and the driver tried his best to help, so who could I be mad at? She was simply on the way home, and it was an accident.

I could not be mad that no one stopped, because the person behind her stopped. The ambulance was there in minutes. The only thing I could really blame was the deer.

I thought of killing deer, but it wasn't their fault. It was just bad luck. Freak accident. I wished that the car needed a recall that we hadn't been notified of. Something, anything, so that I could be pissed. But there wasn't anything. I even wished the accident had been my fault. Then I would have had someone to blame.

The perfect woman died stupidly. End of story.

"Thanks, Universe."

What did the universe do then? It made me live another couple of years without her. I was drinking myself to death, but it wasn't the booze that did me in. Nope, and well, I'm not dead yet, but the cancer would have happened anyway.

It pissed me off that she'd died first. Sorry if I keep jumping around, I'll try to do better. Okay, I'd just said this amazing line, and the kid paused for a second, and I was ready for a fight and what did this girl do?

She was tall, and she had coal-black hair, very long and quite striking. I was sure she wanted me. They all did, but she'd actually said it. What did she do, while Todd was looking at me? She kicked him in the balls. He doubled over. She grabbed the keys out of his hand and said, "Get in, old man."

"What the hell, I'm gonna die sometime," I said, as I headed for the car. Todd lay on the ground moaning, holding his balls. She kicked him in the head and tossed me the keys.

"It's my car and I don't like driving. Let's go."

"Man, you leave her alone," Todd moaned and I ignored him.

I walked over to the passenger side and she looked at me funny. I reached down and opened the door for her.

"Thank you," she said getting in.

I wasn't sure anyone else had noticed, but I imagine it looked pretty cool. It might have looked even better if the car's top had been down.

I walked around the car as Todd got up. He pulled out a flick-knife and shoved it at my leg. Luckily, I noticed in time. I stomped on his hand until he let go and picked up the knife.

"Not a bad knife, kid. Thanks," I said. I closed the knife and put it in my pocket.

I started the car, listening to the engine rev up. I hoped that I hadn't hurt my POS's feelings. It was a crap car, but it had gotten me where I wanted to go.

"Where to?" I asked as I pulled out of her parking place, looking at Todd who was leaning against my POS, holding his hand and rubbing his balls. I thought about tossing him my keys, but the POS deserved better than Todd.

She stayed silent for a while and finally said, "Any place, just get me away from this damn town."

She reached for the control of the top as we stopped at a light.

"Okay, my place first to pick up a few things. How do you feel about the west coast? I've always wanted to drive across the country," I said.

It had been something that Pam and I had planned on but I'd never made the time. I'd spent more vacation days working than traveling. I was glad for all we had done, but the road trip and seeing the world had been our dream. Perhaps it was finally time.

Did I feel like I was giving up on life? Well, as you'll find out, darlin', I fought hard to survive. So no, I didn't feel like this was giving up. It was a lovely diversion.

CHAPTER 1
ROAD TRIP

I have always had a special passion for road trips. Pam and I took several short jaunts before life happened, but our dream had been this cross-country trip, and while I wasn't traveling with her now, I felt that she was near.

Jenny turned off my television and frowned, "What kind of person does not have a working television?"

"I'm sorry, I've always been more of a reader."

She turned and put her hands behind her back like some boss watching her workers, "Alright, everything packed? Thank you for the extra clothes. We can stop for more on the road."

She leaned back and did an exaggerated stretch mimicking one I had done earlier.

I like road trips, but it had been a long time, and I wanted to get the kinks out of my back before we left.

"I'm ready, do you have your pacifier?" I asked, wanting to throw the age thing back at her.

"You have one for me, don't you?" she shot back at lightning speed. That stopped me. I didn't know what to say. She turned and sat down on the bed beside the suitcase, moving up and down a few times, smiling and added, "Springs look like they would work."

"You win. Let's go. We can talk on the road and decide if we're getting one room or two."

It was still warm outside, so we headed for the interstate. The map app on my phone said it was a thirty-nine-hour drive. We had all the time in the world. There was one of those emergency broadcasts alerts on the radio that they ran if there was extreme weather on the way. I quickly turned it off. I didn't want it blow our eardrums.

"Those alerts are too damned loud!" I cursed.

We took the 81 south until just after Johnson City.

"Have you been out west before?" I asked, as we drove with the wind blowing her hair back. She used my phone to play some tunes, loud, and she'd found an old pair of mirrored sunglasses of mine and was wearing them now. If this wasn't paradise, I'm not sure what was.

"No, I've never been out of the state. Well, maybe when I was little, but after my father died, I had to stay home and take care of my mom. She passed a few years later and I have been on my own since," she said, as she took off her shoes and put her bare feet on the dash.

You know that's dangerous, I thought, but I didn't want to get the old man treatment, so I stayed silent.

My phone was pulling double duty. We were using the map app and playing music. She took some time to create a special on-the-road playlist. Before we'd left, she had stomped on her phone and thrown it in the trash.

Seeing that, I had a feeling ours was going to be a wonderful relationship. She was beautiful sitting there feet up, and I could just imagine her taking her top off when it got dark.

"You like looking, don't you?" she said, playfully bringing me back to reality.

I ignored this and turned up the music. Turned out she was a classic rock fan. Or she put it on especially for me. We listened to 'I Wanna Rock' by Twisted Sister. Both of us sang along as loud as we could. Neither one of was especially in tune, but we were having fun.

We drove down to Marion. We exited the interstate and got on Route 11, a secondary road. It was a comfortable drive with the heat on and the top up as it got dark, comfortable for her. But I needed to stop. I was good for about five hours on the road before I needed a break.

We found a small gas station, with a diner attached. She went to pay for the gas while I pumped.

"I got this one, Nick. You get the next tank. I need to go in and pay with cash so just put thirty in," she said, pulling her shoes over her bare feet, and re-tying her top. She had given me a nice show and if I had to die, this was definitely the way to go.

I tipped my virtual hat at her and watched her go inside. I had to laugh. It had been over four hours and I had not thought about the damned doctor once.

The pump made a noise, so I started pumping. When I'd finished I pull up to the front. Before I went inside, I saw a little bit of blood, and maybe hair on the ground. The hair was short, and since it was hunting season, I didn't pay much attention. This could have been a check-in station, for all I knew.

There was no-one behind the register, and at first, I couldn't see Jenny. Looking around the checkout, I grabbed a bag of candy and a diet soda and put them on the counter. Thinking about the drive ahead, I grabbed another one of each. With this combination of chocolate and diet soda, I could go on the road forever.

I heard something, a little choking sound, turned and noticed the top of Jenny's head above one of the aisle dividers. I hadn't seen her before because of all the chips on the top, but there she was looking down and not moving.

While I'm not the most observant person in the world, really, I was just trying to get something to drink and be ready to hit the road again. It didn't take me long to notice that something was wrong.

I had my hand in my pocket, clutching Todd's knife. Rounding the aisle, the first thing I saw was blood, lots of blood. There was a body slumped at Jenny's feet. Laying face up on the ground. Blood and gore on the bags of chips all around it. *Shotgun blast to the chest and face,* I guessed.

I put my hand on her shoulder. She turned and wrapped her arms around me, shaking.

"It's okay kid, I've got you."

She stiffened at that. I knew that endearments and other expressions changed from one generation to the next. What was once fine, was now no longer politically correct. Perhaps that's why I said it. I did mean it in a bad way. I didn't have long for this earth and I enjoyed her being in my life.

I turned her so that I was holding her with one arm and looked down. Since I hadn't heard any gunshots and Jenny wasn't carrying, I knew she hadn't done the deed. I started looking around when she said, "No, look at the body."

"What?" I asked, following her eyes down. The corpse's legs and arms were moving.

"What the fuck?" I said and she giggled. I wondered if she was in shock when she laughed out through her giggles, just catching her breath enough to say, "That's what I said. Jinx."

I'd heard that expression before. I smiled at her the same way I'd smiled at others when I didn't understand the language.

Pulling her back behind me I moved forward, and she grabbed me by my belt, "Please, no!"

"I have to check and see how this person can still be alive. I can't see how they can be alive, but if we can help, we should."

Maybe put them out of their misery.

Bending over the body, every horror movie I had ever seen flashed through my mind. I remembered those scenes where I would say, "I will never do something that stupid."

I remembered coroners talking about bodies moving after death, just before they were eaten or killed. I remember a movie in which the heroine lay under a sheet with a body that farted. The memory made me smile and brought me back to reality.

Most of the blast had gone through the middle of the chest and towards the neck. Everything had exploded outward. Whoever had shot this person had done so from behind.

The legs were moving in a weird rhythm, as if they were attempting a shuffling-type walk, even as it was laying down. If I'd stood up the body, it would have walked.

The hands slowly clenched into fists and let go and clenched again, grabbing at something unseen. I made sure to stay out of reach as I moved to the side, leaving Jenny where she was.

"Keep an eye out," I whispered to her, as I bent over to look at the face.

It was a man, at a guess about twenty years old. Judging by the bits of vest that were still on him, I figured he was the cashier. The neck was almost gone, but a little bit of bone, muscle and other things I didn't know held it on. The bottom jaw was gone, and the upper row of teeth lay exposed.

As I looked down, I felt like I was being watched. His eyes had locked on mine, and his tongue started going around and around the empty space where his mouth had been. He reached out for me and I backed away.

"How did the pump get on?" I asked moving back to Jenny.

"I used to work at one of these and when I didn't see anyone, I turned it on for you. I thought about just doing gas and go but wanted to grab a few things. Is he alive?"

"I don't see how. I'm not a physician, but I have been hunting and I'm fairly sure that his heart was one of the things that were disintegrated by the shots."

I walked past her and put my arm around her waist. We moved to the end of the aisle and turned into the next one. There were no more bodies. We walked towards the diner. I wanted to see if anyone else was hurt or in the same state as our friend on the floor.

There were a few empty seats, a counter with a plate of

doughnuts covered by glass, and what looked like an apple pie. I walked behind the counter and made sure I carefully checked for any movement. Jenny stayed at the counter and waited for me.

I didn't see anyone on the other side of the delivery windows. I tried to push the door to the back open, but something was obstructing it.

"Keep watch," I told Jenny as I crawled through a delivery window.

This is gonna suck, I thought as I pictured every monster movie I'd ever watched, images of a person's head getting chopped off or eaten, as they crawled through something they should have just let go. But I needed to know.

Murder? But how are they still moving? Drugs maybe?

As I got halfway through the delivery window, I could see what was blocking the door. A man dressed in hunting gear, wearing good boots and a red vest, was leaning against the door. His face, or what's left of his face, was splattered against the metal. Had I looked at the other side, I bet I would have seen the little lumps the pellets had made.

The shotgun lay by his side. I had no doubt that this was self-inflicted. I was halfway through and could make a choice to go forward or back, and I remembered someone saying, always go forward.

Right now that was stupid advice, but I did.

I made it through the window without something chopping my head off, and without falling. I waved at Jenny to let her know I was okay. "Be right back. Call out, if you see or hear anything."

I should have packed my guns.

I'm not sure why I hadn't. Maybe I didn't trust the girl and didn't want to give her something to shoot me with late at night, but for whatever reason, my guns were over four hours away.

Thankfully, this body wasn't moving. The head was completely gone. I picked up the shotgun, wiped the blood off, and carefully checked to see how many shells were left. Most hunting shotguns held three shells. if the shooter removed the plug, this gun could hold five. It had two shells left.

"Two shots for the cashier, and one for yourself," I said aloud. Not thinking. I am used to being alone and talking to myself more out of habit.

"What?" Jenny whispered.

"Nothing. Be there in a minute."

I searched his body and found three more shells. *Five shells*, I thought, making a mental note.

Looking him over I noticed a large bite mark, several bite marks on his arm. *They look human.*

I pulled him back, and to the side, careful to not get any blood on myself. I opened the door and went back towards Jenny. She was watching me carefully.

"Phone working?" I asked.

And she shook her head and said, "Fast busy sound."

"I don't know what's going on, but seeing the hunter was bit, my thinking is that the cashier bit the customer. The customer went back out to his truck after punching and pushing the cashier back. He went to his truck, grabbed his shotgun, and came in through a back door. Maybe through the kitchen. He caught the cashier in the aisle shuffling along and shot him. As to why he shot himself?"

I stopped talking I hadn't told her about the hunter yet.

"He shot himself?" she asked, eyes wide. Fear or excitement, I wasn't sure.

"Yes, and as for why, maybe he figured the cashier had some type of infection, or maybe he started feeling bad or hungering to bite people and decided to take the quick way out. Grab some supplies, quickly, and let's get out of here. Once in your car, we'll check the radio and hopefully find out what's going on."

Jenny grabbed some bags while I looked around to make sure there no one else was in here. She went behind the counter and came out with what looked like a small 38 caliber revolver. I was impressed that she knew how to check it was loaded.

"Five shots," she said.

I saw the hunter's truck outside. The gun rack was empty. The passenger's side door was only half-closed. There was a little blood on the ground.

Opening the door, I wasn't sure who surprised whom, but next thing I knew, I had four clawed feet hitting me in the chest. Some type of Pitbull leaped from the truck. He must have been sleeping. Brushing myself off, I let out the laugh I had been holding in for a while, and it turned into hysterical laughter as Jenny started running after the dog, calling for it to come back.

I found more shells on the seat and floor. I didn't take time to count them as I shoved them into my jacket pocket a handful at a time.

Jenny had given up on the dog and met me at the car. She had flipped the gas pump on again. I opened the car's gas cap and topped off the tank. Jenny carried a gas can out of the back of the hunter's truck. I filled that up and put it in the trunk. *It might help in a pinch.*

CHAPTER 2
AM RADIO

She had tried the phone in the diner. Once in the car, I tried my cell. I had a bad habit of leaving it attached to whatever vehicle I was in, so there'd been no way to try before.

It really didn't do us a lot of good. "Please try your call again. The party is not answering."

If there hadn't been something strange going on, I wouldn't have been surprised that the service was down in the mountains, but as it was it I wondered how widespread this was.

There was no traffic on Route 11. It was late so that' wasn't a huge surprise, but still, I would have thought we would see some traffic.

As we drove, I told her, "We will take this back until we hit Interstate 81 and see what traffic looks like there. For now, flip through the radio to see what's there."

There weren't a lot of radio stations down this way, and there was only music on the FM band, "Long cool woman…," one song went. "He wanted 13 but got 31," played on another station. We even tuned in to a cover of a song with the hook, "There stands the glass." It reminded me of my youth when my father had played the original on his phonograph, winding it up, making sure not to overwind. Hearing the scratchy lyrics, I wasn't sure which of my brothers got the phonograph... *Well, their kids would have it now*, I thought.

"Shit, nothing on," she brought me back to the present.

"Flip over to AM," I said to a blank expression, forgetting how young she was. I adjusted the radio while explaining the different types of signals, and told her that I thought, in any case, most FM was automated these days, while AM ran live shows and news programs.

On the first couple of stations, we got an emergency broadcast warning, "....indoors. Do not mix with people you do not know. Do not open the door. Stay indoors," it said, over and over.

The broadcast listed some counties, but I didn't know enough about south Virginia to know which county was which.

"There is a curfew in effect. All interstate traffic has been closed by the governor. Emergency order to shelter in place at George Wythe High School in Wytheville VA," another broadcast said.

"I remember seeing a sign for Wytheville. Let's try there," I said, as we continued to drive. I downshifted into one of the turns and felt her hand on top of mine. It felt nice and I needed human contact.

She flipped through other stations, but they were all playing the same loop. One said the governor would be speaking at 8am.

We drove towards the interstate. It was very quiet. I didn't see any traffic on 81, north or south. We passed a couple of fast-food places, but they were closed and there was no one on the road.

I was about to turn onto 81 North and head towards home, when Jenny pointed to the horizon. There were lights blazing across the entire interstate. Usually, you would see this if someone was working on one lane or the other, but this seemed like some type of checkpoint.

Not really being in the mood to explain why we had guns

belonging to someone dead, I figured it was better to stay on Route 11, drive into Wytheville and park someplace, then walk up to the school. Check out the situation.

Where was that? The roadblock? You are right, that was at Smyth Safety Rest area. I'm not sure you would have heard what happened there. It was horrible. We only found out about it much later, but I believe we were lucky we didn't try the 81 that night. Thinking back, it was a school bus, right? Kids coming back late from a game, and like us, not sure what had happened.

I think that tensions were high because the military had been given a little more information and since no one was ready for this it wasn't a surprise that innocents were killed. Yes, yes I know, if they had done what they were told and not caused a scene, I think that the military would have noticed those things walking out of the woods.

I don't know what you want to call them… I have heard some people call them ghouls, wraiths, and other things. For me, I believe that people just didn't want to call them what they were.

I'm getting ahead of myself. Damn, I'm sorry. I should erase this tape and start again. No, ever forward and all that. Where was I…? Yes, luckily, we took the 11 up to Wytheville. It was eerie driving into town. All the street and traffic lights were off. Not a home in sight had a light on.

At the time I wondered how long something like this had been going on without us knowing, and really since neither of us had been listening to any news for the previous twelve hours, I guess things had happened fast.

It was limited to the southern areas in VA, Kentucky, and North Carolina at first. It had started at a military base. That was what I heard. Another rumor going around, was that it had been a terrorist attack, but that was later.

I drove slowly. Both of us kept our eyes open. I saw the sign for the school as we passed a golf course.

"We'll park at the course and walk over. See what's up," I told Jenny.

"What about the guns?" she asked, as we got out of the car.

"We take them with us. When we get close, we find a place to hide them. Maybe a sand trap or something."

We headed across the course. I've never been a golfer and laughed, since I knew I should be wearing different shoes on the precious grass. Looking around as we walked, we didn't see anyone. We passed a lake, but I didn't hear any frogs, crickets, or birds.

Stopping at the last sand trap before the school, I said, "Look around and look from all directions where we are. Mark this in your memory. The car is that way. I'm putting the keys and the guns here."

I had grabbed a towel from the trunk and wrapped the guns and keys in it. I didn't want to have to deal with sand later.

She hugged me and gave me a quick kiss on the lips. It surprised me, but I think she was telling me, 'If you keep me safe, I'll give you a reward.'

But that's just me, a cynical old man talking.

We walked a dozen or so yards to the right before moving forward. I didn't want anyone who might have seen us near the school figure where we'd come from, to protect that sand trap and the car.

Climbing a low hill, we could see the school and the football field. There were lights on, and several small fires in barrels marked the road. A couple of road flares, almost burnt out, had been set up to indicate where people should park.

It seemed like the first group that had arrived had been orderly, but the later ones didn't even shut their doors. A few still had the dome lights on with the batteries draining.

We walked past these vehicles and didn't see anyone inside, nor in the cars ahead of us.

I spotted a police officer outside the school. Well, he looked like a police officer who was turning a corner to head to the other side of the school. I was going to call out, but didn't.

The door was locked, but I could see someone on the other side with their back turned to us. I knocked gently, and they didn't notice. I knocked harder.

The back of the jacket read Wytheville Sheriff's Department, and we both relaxed. That was until he, well it, turned around. It saw us and pushed straight into the door. It was fast. The door pushed outward, but the chain on the inside held. We could see its face in the window as its teeth kept chomping at the air. Almost as if it could smell us. Its tongue danced around inside its mouth the same way as that of the cashier. I could see the saliva running down the window as his tongue swirled around.

I stepped back and accidentally knocked Jenny to the ground. Bending over to help her up was the only thing that saved me. The other officer, the one who'd been outside, had come back, made a grab for me. He missed and tripped over my legs as I was bent over.

"Fuck me," I said, grabbing Jenny's arm and yanking her to her feet.

"Go, go, go!" I shouted to her, seeing officer 1 getting up, and hearing officer 2, its chomps now joined by others and the chain creaking against the weight of them.

We ran for the sand trap. The zombie. Yes, I know, not a politically correct term, but let me review. No real sign of intelligence. Eats people, especially the brain and is hard as fuck to kill. That is a zombie or any action hero from the 80's. I wonder if any of them made it?

It wasn't gaining on us. They were quick for the first strike. Like a Venus flytrap. They struck quickly, but for the long haul we humans were faster.

I was holding back as I ran.

"Jenny, you get the guns out. I'm going to try and distract it. When you have them, let me know and I'll come and shoot it."

"I know how to shoot," she yelled back and that answered that question. When she got to the sand trap, I yelled a couple of things that you would never yell if you weren't running from a zombie, and waved my arms.

It turned towards me, and I kept it moving around the sand trap. I noticed that the doors from the school were open, and it looked like there had been a lot of people in the gym.

Reports later said three hundred and seventy-five souls. I kind of like how people said it like that. Anyway, when we came round again, I saw Jenny had her gun up. I turned and yelled, "Boo!" at the zombie, and I'll be damned if it didn't stop for a second to look at me. Well, there was some intelligence there.

Jenny shot and the first one hit it in the shoulder. She pumped in another round as it turned and started shambling towards her, the second shot hit it in the face, and it went down. We didn't hang around to investigate its legs moving. We grabbed the second gun and keys and ran for the car. Behind us, we heard more of them coming, but the chain had given us a little time.

As we approached the clubhouse, an old man stepped out, evidently hearing the noise. Dressed in short green pants, a white-collar shirt and golf shoes, he carried a golf club. He didn't carry it to attack. Rather, he, or it, dragged it behind him, as if he was going to play a round.

Its mouth chomped at us. Its tongue did the circle. I shot it with the revolver while on the run. The first shot hit it in the shoulder. It kept coming. The second bullet went in the neck and it still kept coming with the same chomping and sucking sound. The third hit it between the eyes. When it went down, it was like someone had flipped a switch. First moving, then down. I grabbed the golf club as we went by. I only had a few shots left for the revolver. I needed another weapon.

Once in the car, we headed out of the parking lot as the first zombies tripped over the chain for the driveway. It was one of those chains made to guide people on where to park, but four zombies hit it at the same time and went down. *Not the smartest things, thankfully,* I thought.

I didn't want to go further into town or hit the interstate, so I backtracked some and took a turn that said something lake. I couldn't remember the name, but I thought that if there was a lake, there might also be cabins to hole up in for the night.

CHAPTER 3
PLAYING HOUSE

The drive wasn't bad. We didn't see anything trying to kill us, and most of the homes we passed had either blacked out their windows or had the lights off. The radio was on a loop talking about the governor's broadcast scheduled for the next morning.

A sign pointed towards a main office as we followed a driveway up and around the lake.

Several cabins sat beside the lake and like the houses we had passed, were in darkness. Figuring one was just as good as the others, I drove to the last one and backed the car into the empty driveway.

I hadn't seen any cars at the other cabins and told Jenny that if we ended up staying, I would move the car down to the parking lot, so that no one passing by would know we were in one of the cabins.

"Why not park it here?" she asked.

"One of the major problems in situations like this are people. There are good ones, but there are also looters and people just trying to survive… like us. People who have no business being where they are," I said, and went on to say that hopefully, we would hear some good news in the morning.

"For now, let's check out the cabin."

She kept the shotgun. I had reloaded it, showing her how, and gave her some additional shells. I was carrying the revolver and the golf club. I walked up to the front door, moved her to one side and myself to the other, and knocked gently. I didn't hear anyone inside and knocked again, calling out, "Hi, we're not bad people, and we're still alive. Anyone in there? If so, we will try the next cabin."

I waited for a bit and nothing. Moved to the windows and put my face against the glass. This was a scary thing for me. I could picture someone seeing my face and blasting it, but nothing bad happened. I repeated my message tapping on the window.

The cabin had two windows in front on either side of the door. We moved around the cabin and didn't see anything or anyone. The moon was out, and I could see fairly well, so we kept the flashlight off - a small one she had on her keychain, better than nothing.

Seeing something hanging in the air, I reached up. It was a cable. Not a power cable, but something else. Jenny switched her torch on. It was a zip line.

"This could have been a fun trip, if not for the… you know, zombies," I whispered to her.

The back door was shut and there was no response. There were three hooks for the zip line hanging on the back wall. I assume they were called hooks, maybe pulleys. Either way, the general direction of the line appeared to take you to the lake that was a few hundred yards down the hill.

"I'd love to know what is at the end of this line. Tomorrow, we check that out."

"I'm not a baby," she said, and it surprised me. Looking at her carrying a shotgun, standing beside the back door to a cabin we didn't own, I looked at her questioningly.

"Just don't assume that I'm in this with you till the end. Okay, I will let you lead for now, but If I think you are making the wrong decision, I'm out," she said quickly, and I wondered how long she had been holding that back.

I let out a small laugh, I hadn't realized I'd been holding. You know, if you think of it, it was kinda funny. Here I was with a woman a half of my age, just twelve hours or so after I had been told I was dying.

"I understand. We will talk things out. For now, we play it my way. If you have a better idea, I'm all ears," I said and that seemed to satisfy her.

I checked the doors and door frames for spare keys. I also checked to see if the windows were unlocked. I noticed that the shutters could close. They would not hold things off for a long time, but they would at least block the light, once we get inside. But I couldn't find any keys.

I grabbed a towel and our luggage from the car. There wasn't much of use, but we had a change of clothes and if someone took the car, they didn't get everything we had. I hoisted the gas can out of the trunk. I went around the back of the cabin, took the towel, held it up to one of the glass panes and hit it with the golf club. The sound of the glass breaking was minimal, but the piece that hit the floor inside was loud. If something else was in there, we would have heard it.

I unlocked the window and started to climb up. "It's easier if I go," she said, and while I agreed, it didn't seem very alpha male to me. She shone her light inside. We couldn't see anything. I took the revolver so that she could climb easier. When she was inside, I handed it back to her so she could at least shoot a few times if anything moved. Then duck while I shot from the window with the shotgun. That's what was going on in my head.

The strategizing was un-needed and no one and no zombies were inside. She opened the back door. I closed the window shutters of the broken window and latched them from the inside.

She re-locked the door while I carried our stuff over to the table in the center of the cabin. The cabin had a very simple layout, a large open room that had the kitchen, kitchen table, and living room area that took you to the front door, with two adjacent rooms. One room, the larger one, had a bathtub and shower combination, and thankfully, an indoor toilet. My assumption was this was a cabin for couples and or people with just a couple of kids. Everything looked like it worked, but since the electricity was off, I couldn't be sure. The breakers were on, but there was no power.

"I bet they turn it off until people check-in," I said.

The refrigerator was open. It had a fridge and freezer, and the previous occupants or the cleaners had left it open to air out. I closed the doors to have them out of the way. There was water to the sink, and the stove ran on propane. The tank was outside.

We quickly moved through the cabin taking every door the way I'd seen police do in movies. This method of entry wasn't required, but perhaps it was good practice. After we were sure there was no one or nothing in the cabin, we closed the shutters and latched them.

The cabin did have a couple of battery-powered lanterns, with the solar charger on them and cranks to charge. They also had a radio that had a hand crank and a solar power charger.

I went outside and told her through the door to turn one of the lights on. Then had her turn it off. We did this several times while I went around filling in any cracks where the light was coming out with mud or leaves. It wasn't perfect, but after laying down our survival towel at the base of the front door and another we found in the cabin over the back door, hardly any light escaped the cabin.

"Okay, we are home for the night. Let's see what we have to eat," I said, sitting down. I expected her to take her own seat at the table. It seated four, but she came over to me, motioned me to turn the chair out a little, and sat on my lap. She wrapped her arms around my neck and, burying her face on my chest, started to shake. I put my arms around her and... Well, don't worry about what I said to her. Okay, just know that sex was the last thing on my mind with the world crashing down around us, but having her on my lap did make me happy and I'm not sorry about that. Hopefully you understand.

Damn, where was I? Okay so the rest of the night was a mixture of kissing a little bit. Mainly to kiss the tears away. I wanted her to get some sleep in one of the bedrooms, but she wouldn't be away from me, so I sat on the couch. She laid her head on my lap and after a while, she went to sleep. I told her that I would wake her up in a few hours so she could keep watch.

I turned the lights off. I combined a lot of things into my backpack. I didn't want us having to carry the old suitcase I had given Jenny that had once belonged to Pam.

We had made a plan - if something happened we would go out the back, run around the side to the car and head out. If that wasn't an option, we would go for the zip line and take our chances on what was below.

As it turned out, she was a sound sleeper, so I just let her sleep while I rested my eyes. Years ago, I had worked at a dispatch center for an electrical company. Our nightshift motto was, "We may doze, but we never close!" and I found that I could get a good half-sleep, but still be able to wake up if I heard anything.

I didn't hear anything, and she stirred as the sun was coming up. She looked up at me, my hand gently brushing her hair. I must have started that while sleeping. Damn, I'm an old sap. Anyway, her eyes shining up at me made me smile.

"I'm glad I found you," I said, not thinking of anything other than how happy I was at that moment.

I mean, fuck, I was dying, so for me, it didn't matter if the rest of the world was going to shit. I couldn't think of a better place to be than this cabin with a beautiful young woman.

She rolled over onto her back, looked up at me and asked, "Tell me about your life before, and why you decided to run away with me yesterday?"

I told her some of it. How I had been married with lots of plans to travel, but life had happened, and we had ended up in a rut until my wife passed. Me not knowing any better, I just kept working. When I saw her and Todd, I couldn't let him hit her.

"He used to do it a lot," she said, "I don't know why I let him. I guess it was because my mama let my stepdad hit her. He even hit me. But there was something about today. I think when I saw you, the look in your eyes gave me courage."

She giggled and said, "You looked so pissed off, was it all Todd?"

"No, I just had dealings with another asshole earlier and with any luck, I will never see him again. Let's see what we can figure out for breakfast, then move the car. We have enough food to last a couple of days and once we know what the governor says… You know I didn't vote for that guy … Anyway, once we see what he has to say, we will plan from there."

To keep me from talking politics and perhaps because she liked me, she leaned up, giving me her first real kiss. Neither of us thought about the fact that we had morning breath. We just held each other, not moving, just kissing and holding each other.

I whispered, "Breakfast can wait."

And she whispered back breathlessly. "Are there mattresses on any of the beds?"

There were mattresses and we even found sheets in the dressers. We took time to brush our teeth and I let her freshen up. We were both quiet, but it was very passionate and I'm sorry to say that I fell in love with her a little bit and later felt guilty because my wife had passed away too early.

Afterward, we lay listening to the radio. FM stations were still playing music. *It will do that until the batteries run out or the generators die,* I thought, but I didn't mention it to Jenny. We lay there in each other's arms, listening to the sounds around us, relaxing in the calm before the storm we knew was on the way.

CHAPTER 4
HOWDY NEIGHBOR

The governor's speech wasn't anything special. It sounded like it had been recorded. There were no questions taken, and it was very dry. He said things like "Shelter in place. Do not go outside." and "The CDC is working on a cure." If we had learned anything from Covid we knew that the CDC didn't really do that. They coordinated with different pharmaceutical companies, but all in all, I didn't have a good feeling.

"They don't know a lot, do they?" Jenny said.

"No, I don't think they do. We'll stay here for a few days, and then try to make it back home. You should have seduced me a day earlier and we would still be home," I said. I meant this to be a cute throwaway line to make her smile, but it really made both of us think more about how close we were to death.

"It will be OKAY!" I emphasized the *okay*, to make her know I meant it, "Darlin', I do not have anything left, but I will give all I have to find you someplace safe. I promise."

"Why?" she asked.

I shrugged, wrapped my arms around her. Holding her and taking in her scent, trying to recapture the happy feeling we'd had.

She went about organizing our belongings in the backpack. We had done a good job the night before, but I wanted her to have something to do while I checked out the zip line and moved the car.

Stepping outside, I heard her lock the door. She had the keys to the car and we agreed where to meet if something happened at the cabin. We agreed on a couple of spots and times, so if the first one wasn't possible, hopefully the second one would be.

Too much planning, but hopefully we don't need it, I thought as I walked down the hill. Taking the zip line was an option, but I didn't want anyone to see me flying through the trees, plus it would stink if halfway down I saw that the bottom was full of zombies.

I know you don't like that word. I'm sorry, but what else do we call them?

The zip line ran to the bottom of the hill and the shore of the lake. I took the direct route and kept an eye on where it went. The line zigzagged back and forth. I guessed it wouldn't be all that fast.

It stopped at the bottom of the hill by the lake. The lake was beautiful, framed by sand. The zip line ended twenty feet before a dock. A large pole was set up with a couple of cushions on them. While it wasn't a professional rig, it was very nice.

No one and nothing was on the beach. Walking out to it, I made sure that my footprints came from the side. It took me a little bit of walking back up the hill and around, but as humans easily turned predators, I didn't want to take a path leading straight back.

The dock was short, just far enough in the water so that you could step onto a boat and float out. The water by the dock was only two or three feet deep. The boats looked like they could hold three or four people. Wide enough for two to sit in the middle, with one in front and one at the back.

They were chained to a rack, but it didn't take much effort to get them loose. They looked in good shape and had paddles.

I unchained them, one less thing to do if we were in a hurry to leave. I thought about hiding one of the boats, but figured if someone else got it, they needed it as much as we did.

I scanned across the lake for a road or a trail where I could park the car. *Not the best type of vehicle for this type of trip, but it would work,* I thought as I walked back up the trail. I could see evidence of others using this path. A couple of trees were bent over from people pulling on them to climb up the trail.

"Bet this place was fun when it was alive," I said aloud, not thinking. When you lived alone as long I had, you sometimes talked to yourself, which wasn't surprising.

The response, "Yes, it was" did surprise me.

I didn't reach for the revolver in my pants' pocket. Its bulge was covered by the T-shirt I was wearing, and I didn't want to give anything away.

"Just stay where you are. Stand up straighter if you would. So that Richard can get a shot if you don't listen or if you're one of them," a man said. I couldn't see him.

I did as I was told and noted how he referred to the zombies for future reference. One of them.

"I'm Nick, and I'm here by myself. If that's your cabin up there, I'll clear out," I said.

"Well, I'll tell your friend what you think of her, but I commend you for trying to protect her. I'm Wesley, my son Richard has you covered. Please let me know why I should not have him shoot you," he said, still not stepping out where I could see him. They'd been watching me for a while and I hadn't heard them. *Guess I wasn't as good in the woods as I thought I was.*

They hadn't tried to harm her, or I would have heard the shotgun. That made me feel a little better.

"I would like to tell you why, I really would, but if I was in your situation with a son to protect, I think I would shoot first and ask questions later. The only problem with that is that we are only a day into whatever's going on. There could still be police and military to answer to. So, ask me again in a day or two and I'll have a better answer," I said, while brushing grass from my hands, wiping it on my pants.

I wanted them to get used to seeing me move. I doubt I could kill both with the two shots I had left, but maybe I could get a warning shot off for Jenny.

Wesley started to laugh and stepped from behind a near-by tree. I couldn't see clearly, but my assumption was he was holding a semi-automatic handgun. He lowered the gun and holstered it.

"The cabin you're in, it's my uncle's. Ours is the one just in front. We saw you drive up last night and didn't recognize you. We wanted to see what you were up to. I liked how your first instinct was to check out the exits. I assume your next move is to move the car," he said, as if he had read my mind.

I smiled saying, "And if you have a Burger King nearby, I may go there for lunch."

We both laughed, and he looked at me. His eyes were dead. "My son means more to me than you, her, or anyone else on the planet. I'll kill you in a heartbeat if it saves him."

"I understand and feel the same about the girl. Her name's Jenny," I said and turned slowly as Wesley motioned for Richard to come out.

I smiled. Richard didn't have a pistol, rifle, or shotgun. He had an old-style hunting slingshot, the kind you used with pellets. He had it armed and ready to go. Basically, you held the shot in the little cup made from leather or rubber. You held it loosely to keep the projectile in place. Then you pulled back and the band stretched. You aimed and fired.

As a kid, I could hit a metal gate over a hundred yards away and penetrate a watermelon at fifteen paces.

"I like it," I said, nodding towards the weapon.

"Thanks, mister, dad got it for me last year, and we practice all the time."

He smiled that awkward smile that boys twelve or thirteen have. A man, but not yet a man.

I loved the implied threat and smiled, "We have food, not enough for long, but I figured on making a run somewhere for supplies in a few days. How're you for food?" I asked easily. I knew it was a touchy subject. He wouldn't want to give too much away.

"We're in the same boat as you. I think if we pool our food, we four could last two weeks on what we have, but we should try to get food as soon as possible. Who knows how long this is going to last?"

"Did you hear the governor…" I didn't get out the entire word before Wesley spat on the ground and cussed our wonderful Virginia governor. I liked him more.

We made our way up the mountain. They hadn't heard anyone else, and I was amazed at how quiet they were in the woods. I thought I was good, but they were really good watching out for twigs, and leaves as they walked.

Wesley, noticing me watching his son pick out the path, said, "We come out here all the time. Ever since his mom passed, it's been our weekend get-away. We play soldiers and army. All the fun stuff I did as a kid. Capture the flag, and whatever else we can think of. He told me he might want to go into the service someday, so I figured it wouldn't be a bad idea to teach him as much as I could."

He smiled as he watched his son walk up the hill.

I let them have me in the middle, and I hadn't pulled out my pistol. I think that Wesley saw it, but he didn't say anything. Sometimes you just got a good feeling about people, and I had that about them.

Richard held up his hand with a military-style gesture to stop us moving. Then he held two fingers to his eyes and pointed. We both looked, hoping that it wasn't zombies or the others, whatever he called them. It wasn't. A rabbit cowered on the side of the hill as if the world hadn't ended.

Richard pulled back his slingshot, looked at his father who nodded approval, focused and fired. The rabbit was a good twenty or thirty feet up the hill. If Wesley and I hadn't stopped, it would have run, but as Richard was above us, it must have been waiting.

The shot was true, the rabbit slumped over. "Good shot," I whispered.

I could tell they were both proud of themselves. Father and son. *As it should be.*

Richard picked up the rabbit, making sure it was dead. Never mind how. I've been a hunter and I approved of how he did it. You couldn't just pick up game that looked dead. I've heard of people gored by deer they thought were dead. Richard had been taught right.

We got to the cabin, and I called out quietly, "Jenny, these are friends, and they brought food." I then gave a little whistle that meant it was okay. We had decided that if one of us was being held at gunpoint, anything we would say other than what people told us would make them suspicious. I would only whistle if I was with someone we could trust.

Now the problem is, I can't whistle, but it was an attempt, and she laughed as she opened the door, "You really can't whistle, can you?"

We explained to our new friends what that was about.

We decided that Jenny and Richard would stay in the cabin while Wesley and I moved the car and made a quick food run. He had his semi-automatic, and I told him I only had a few shots for the revolver to which he responded, "Let's stop by the cabin. I have some .38s, I believe. My uncle had one last year. Well, he had his .357 and as you know if you want to save money on ammo you can target shoot with .38's in a 357 revolver."

I did know this, but I appreciated his knowledge.

"Did you always know the woods?"

Richard started laughing. He was drinking a soda that came out of his nose. Seemed he and his father had been trying to quit soda and now that the world was in the state it was in, it was decided he could have one of ours.

Richard just patted his knee and pointed at his dad. "With a name like..." then he laughed and finally said, "With a name like Wesley. Come on man, you are smarter than that. Daddy grew up with silver and gold spoons, as they say. Mom's side of the family liked to hunt and fish and even mom was a crack shot... Anyway, dad is a city feller." He said that with all the grown-up, up-tight voice he could muster and added, "With him being a city feller, he got all his knowledge out of books, and then my uncles on mom's side taught us the rest."

I could tell from Wesley's reaction that he was pleased to see his son laugh again and added, "He's right, I didn't know anything but what I'd played when I was a kid, so when I met his mom at college and found out how much she liked the woods and wilderness I told her I loved it. I made a big thing of saying how good I was in the woods." He smiled at the memory. "And that night I went to a used bookstore and purchased the *Foxfire* book series. If you've ever read them, they are the ones that first teach you everything from dressing a hog, to log cabin building and snake lore. Step-by-step instructions. As you can imagine when we went camping that first time, I was a mess..."

His son, having caught his wind, continued the story, "They took him snipe hunting, can you believe that, mister? Snipes. My uncles took him to the middle of their property, gave him a sack, and said they would drive it to him. That he would feel it run in the sack and should close it as soon as something was in it," he said and tapped his dad on the chest to have him continue.

"They left me out there for four hours. I did find my way back to their house, and Sara hugged me and gave me the best cup of tea I'd ever drank in my life. Super sweet. The kind that makes your toes curl. We were together until just last year. She and her uncles taught me, helped teach Richard all they could before heading overseas."

"Soldiers?" Jenny asked.

"Yes, Mam," Richard said, which earned him a pinch on the arm.

"Call me Jenny, I am not that much older than you," she said.

Richard's frown turned to a smile when she added, "We also have some moon pies. If you like those."

As they were going to be fast friends, we agreed on a new code for entering. I told Jenny to try and keep the smell of the rabbit to a minimum.

"I know you want to make it good, but we don't need the smell of cooking meat drifting all over the place. Try to do something like soup, something you can keep the lid on," I said, heading out. I was a little surprised when she ran over and kissed me.

I didn't mind that there were more of us now, but these were strangers, and affection wasn't something I was used to showing around others.

"Come back to me," she whispered in my ear, before going back inside.

"Top up or down?" I joked with Wesley, as we headed into town.

CHAPTER 5
ZOMBIE FOOD

We decided to try the gas station diner combination that Jenny and I had stopped at before. I'd flipped the sign to closed. Who knew, maybe it'd been left it alone.

We didn't see any traffic on Route 11 after coming down the mountain road. I was kind of hoping to see someone, but nothing. At least, the streets weren't covered in zombies. The FM band still had music, but there were fewer stations now. On AM, there wasn't anything new, so we turned it off.

"You know, if this thing goes on, I'm going to get something besides this convertible. I like it and it's a fun ride, but it's not practical for the end of the world," I said, winding the window down a little. Not much, because I didn't want anything to shove its arm in if I stopped.

Wesley looked at me funny for a second. I guess his sense of humor wasn't the same as mine. *Oh well.*

"Do you really think this is it? I hope not. Not for my sake, but Richard's."

"I know, and I'm not sure. My hope is that this is something localized. Have you noticed how the emergency services don't say, 'Oh California is perfect, or NY is fine, or even Hawaii says

Aloha?' That really concerns me. Anyway, here it is, I can only see the same truck that was here before."

I parked and we went out. The dog was sitting beside the truck, and I motioned for it to come to me, and it took off running. I parked beside the pumps again. Figured we might as well fill up again. I doubted I could get more than a gallon or two in, but better to have than not.

On the way, I'd told Wesley about the lay-out of the shop and what we would be able to get there. Popping the trunk of the Mustang, he grabbed his gas can and set it beside the pump.

The sign still said closed and I couldn't tell if anyone else had been in or not. Wesley had his semi-automatic out, and I had the revolver. I'd never really looked at it to get the name. It was a Ruger. At first, I thought I would be throwing it away when empty, or more likely throw it at a zombie, but as I had six rounds in it and half a box of shells in my pocket, I decided to hang on to it. It wasn't the fastest weapon to reload, but it was better than nothing. I had my trusty golf club in my hand when I opened the door.

It looked the same inside. I wasn't sure if anyone had taken anything off of the shelves. We quickly searched the place and not finding anything alive or newly dead, I turned on the gas pumps. Wesley went out to fill up the car and his can while I checked on something.

The truck owner who had shot himself was still in the kitchen. I checked on Twitch. That was what I'd nicknamed the zombie whose foot had been twitching, and sure enough, it was still going. The tongue was a horrible thing to watch going around and around. I noticed that his arms were moving some as well.

The truck owner was still where I had left him. Searching for his keys wasn't a lot of fun, but I found them. The truck looked to be only about ten years old. There wasn't much that could go wrong with one of these unless they rusted away. That was what usually killed this type of truck.

I turned on the second pump and went outside. Wesley was putting the gas can in the Mustang. I waved at the truck, and he understood. I opened the door to get in and the dog flew past me and into the truck. It turned and sat facing the windshield, as if to say, "Let's go".

I laughed and got in. For a second, I was tense. I hoped that the dog hadn't decided this was its truck and not let me drive, but evidently, he just liked to ride.

I parked by the pumps, got out and left the door open. Figure he could get in or out if he wanted.

We watched the area while filling up the truck. When we were done, I hopped in beside the dog, and Wesley drove the car around the back of the diner.

When I'd been in the kitchen before, I had left the back door open. To the side was a walk-in freezer with a small stock room. I figured it was easier to carry everything out of the back rather than dragging our loot through the store.

We loaded cans and heavy items into the back of the truck, and smaller items into the car. We picked up bags of chips and candy. I know, I know. Candy? But really if the world was ending, why not enjoy the little things? I actually started to pick up a pack of smokes but decided to not be that guy. I did grab a few lighters and extra butane.

I was moving about when Wesley went to open the freezer. I hadn't thought anything of it. When the freezer door started to open of its own accord, I immediately drew my gun. Wesley's eyes turned into saucers, and for a minute he probably thought I'd lost it, but when he saw the arm reaching for him, he was glad I'd pulled my weapon.

Jumping backwards, he tripped over a box he had placed on the floor.

Her hair was long. She was wearing a short waitress uniform, and I think she could have been beautiful at one time. Her name tag said 'Mags'.

You may be wondering how I had time to read her name tag.

Well, she was frozen. As the power was still running in the diner and for the pumps, the freezer was still cold. I couldn't see a bite mark on her as she slowly emerged from the freezer.

She turned to look at me. Her eyes were dead. I knew what had happened. She had a bandage on her arm. The first one who had bitten her, the truck driver, he must have wrapped her wound and then told her to hide in the freezer. It either didn't open from the inside, or the change had happened quickly. I would have to check.

For now, I said, "I'm sorry, Mags," and I shot her between the eyes. I actually was able to place the gun right against her skull. Well, an inch back. But what I wanted to do was verify if a brain shot would kill them.

It did and she dropped like a ton of bricks. Her face was what got me the most. There were scratches on her face, and I could see the flesh she'd pulled off in her hands and mouth. She had been chewing when she'd emerged from the freezer.

"Fuck me," I said to Wesley helping him up, "She froze to death in there and then turned into a zombie and the only food she's had is her own flesh."

"Fuck," we both said in unison.

We didn't find much else in the freezer. We were both a little in shock. As we stepped outside, carrying the last load, neither of us noticed the trucks pull up. Our ears were still ringing from the gunshot. Perhaps they had all pulled up at the same time.

There were four of them. Three were taking stuff out of the back of my truck. The fourth man was standing guard. He had a hunting rifle pointed at the ground in front of his feet. The scope on it was at least a ten-power. That struck me as an odd weapon, but who knew.

"There is plenty to go around," Wesley said. You could tell that he didn't want trouble. The three stopped moving and were just standing there, holding the boxes they had. One spat some type of tobacco on the ground and smiled.

I didn't move. I didn't say anything, wanted to see what they did first. The world was ending. Maybe this was the end times, but it had only been twenty-four hours or so and people couldn't be this crazy.

The leader, well, I assumed he was the boss as he was armed and wasn't doing any work, started to raise the barrel of his weapon. Wesley was still talking, and I really didn't know what he was saying. I was watching the rifle. If the guy was dumb enough to try and use the scope at this range, I could shoot him and reload and shoot him again. Still, he looked like he might try to fire from the hip. doing a point and shoot.

As soon as I saw the gun barrel move up, I noticed Wesley taking step back. I threw the box I had forward, most likely not hard enough to make it to the rifle, but I hoped instinct would take over and the guy would see something flying towards him and back up or stop.

The leader raised his rifle and was about to fire when one of the jars from the box hit the ground and shattered. You could smell pickles instantly. Anyway, he didn't shoot and that extra half-second was all I needed. As soon as I'd pushed the box at him, I drew my revolver. I shot him twice, once in the head, and once in the chest.

Wesley was moving as well. He drew his own gun and shot the second guy in his side before he had a chance to drop his box. The other two took off at a run. I shot them in the back.

Wesley turned on me, pressed me against the wall of the store, and said, "They were running away."

I waited as he kept pushing me against the wall. I could imagine what was going through his mind. The same thing I was sure had gone through mine. But the difference was, I got there first. Then he said, "But running to where, and for what?"

"Exactly," I said while pulling my shirt back into place. "We don't know where they came from or who they were with. I think we should hurry and get out of here."

We took our stuff from their truck and put it back in mine. I grabbed the leader's rifle. He had a box of shells in the front. The gun looked like a .308, but as you know, I wasn't a gun person. The other two had semi-automatics but they weren't in near as good shape as Wesley's. I wondered if they'd been fired before or cleaned after being fired.

We took them because it never hurt to have extra weapons. Wesley drove the car and I opened the door of the truck. The dog was nowhere to be seen. I assumed it had run when they'd opened the door. I called for it, but it didn't come back, and I didn't know its name.

I really hoped it would come back. When it didn't, I took a couple of cans of dog food that I'd grabbed from the shelves in the gas station and opened them, pouring them out on the ground. Figured it would find them.

We agreed to split up. Wesley would go first, and I would follow a few minutes after. If someone were to follow us, we might get lucky and spot them.

No one did, and maybe we just got lucky eluding others. If the guys we'd encountered were part of another group, we didn't want them to know where we were going.

I met Wesley on the road opposite the Slide for Life. We left the truck there, hiding it as best we could, with supplies on board.

"If we have to go, at least we'll have food and water."

We parked in an area that had been logged, to make way for power lines. The way they'd cut across mountains looked awful, but as I now had a four-wheel drive, I thought that a cross-country trip wasn't out of the question.

"Roads? Who needs roads?" I said aloud and we both laughed, having thought the same thing.

"It wouldn't be as easy as a Sunday drive. But I have some fencing tools. If we can open fences up enough to let the truck through and close them behind us, we can camp out where people wouldn't ever think of going. It's been dry lately. I think we could make it."

That was our fallback plan. We would try the main highway

in a few days but if worse came to worst and things went bad at the cabins, then it would be time to get those tires dirty.

We took the car back around and made sure no one followed us. At the top of the hill, I pulled it around the side of the cabin. It was out of sight and this gave us multiple options.

When Jenny opened the door, the smell of food hit me and I realized how hungry I was. We quickly went inside with our haul and unloaded the stuff from the freezer. I figured ice cream for dessert, but left the rest until later.

"Smells wonderful," I said after we were inside, and I noticed Jenny stuffing a towel around the base of the door.

"Figure cut down on some of the smell," she said, walking over and kissing me. "Honey, tell me about your day," she said, mimicking one of the old television show wives.

I looked around and said, "Not until I have my martini and slippers."

We enjoyed supper that night and the next couple of days went well. It wasn't until several weeks later that we found out how bad it was. Wesley or Jenny and I would make quick trips seeing if the roads were open, or if more people were moving, but we didn't see anyone. Either everyone was dead, or people were taking this lockdown a lot more seriously than they had when Covid had first hit.

Listening to the emergency broadcasts was part of our routine. They started broadcasting at 9am, then again at noon and at 5pm. They usually played the same recording with just a little new information thrown in. "Cause remains unknown", "Congress in lockdown", "President and Vice President say help is on the way". These messages sounded like they were designed to pacify people. There was no talk about how widespread the outbreak was.

Several weeks later, we tuned in just after breakfast. This time there was no recording; it was live. We'd long been wondering why we hadn't heard from the president, from Congress, or any other official other than the governor and his staff.

We'd missed the beginning because the broadcast had been the same for so long, "Stay indoors, all will be well. CDC is working on it." But not this time.

Wesley recognized the voice immediately because he had campaigned for the lieutenant governor.

"I am sorry to report that the governor has taken ill. He will be euthanized this afternoon. If anyone is sick with a high fever for more than twenty-four hours, they should be euthanized."

CHAPTER 6
HELL IN A HANDBASKET

Well, you can guess our reaction to that. At first, there was disbelief. Did we hear that right? The government told people to euthanize the sick and authorities would come to collect the remains and take them to state facilities?

It was crazy. Wrap up and leave the bodies on the street, or at your door, he'd said. Y-Group, a combination of several government law enforcement agencies would be picking them up.

Anyone with active symptoms should not be engaged. They should be locked up where they were, or left to the elements. They were no longer family members. They were not friends. They were the infected and there was no cure.

We decided to stay where we were until we'd be forced to move, either by people or the others. We speculated on the best places in the U.S. to survive for long periods of time, and we felt it was better to stay where we were.

Jenny came up with an idea, and I could not fault her for it. "Power, the Internet, phones are all out. We need to go to the library. They might have one in town. And if not they are bound to have one at the school. We need books. We need to know how to survive. Like the *Fox Fire* books Wesley had, and others," she said, looking up at me with eyes that made me sad and happy at the same time.

I was still feeling good at this time. According to fuck head, my doctor, if you remember him, what I had was like a ticking timebomb. I remember he told me, "If left untreated, you will be going along and just die. So you need treatment." And that was when I'd punched him.

Okay, I didn't punch him, but I thought about it.

I couldn't fault her for wanting to find books and wished that there was an electronics store or someplace where we could find a ham radio. My friend's father had had one when I was a kid and he used to talk to people all over the world but getting into it without power was most likely a no-go.

The truck, unfortunately, didn't have a CB radio.

I wanted to leave Jenny and the boy in the cabin, but neither would have any of it. Since this was going to be a long trip, what if we didn't return? Where would that leave them?

We took the convertible and decided that this time we would find a new car. Something with four doors and a roof. There was still plenty of food. We didn't need to make a supply run. Unless someone had found the truck, it was still full of provisions.

On the way, I said, "If things go bad, we turn around and haul ass back to the cabin. If, for some reason, we get separated." I pointed to a couple of places as we drove and said, "Meeting place 3, then 2 and 1," as we got closer to town. I numbered them in reverse order, not knowing if they were safe or not. They were as good a place as any to hide on the roof and wait for whoever had a car.

We hit town about 8am and decided to check out a couple of car dealerships first. We figured normal people would still be asleep, and who knew what schedule zombies were on?

There was no traffic. No one had set up barricades. A couple of cars that had hit light poles and traffic lights, the doors hung open, but no one was in the cars and

"Just strange," Wesley said. "I expected to see more people, bodies, or zombies, or something. The nothingness just makes me think that maybe we missed an evacuation order. If you think of it, that could have been it. Perhaps people were told to get out on the first day and we just missed the word."

What he said made more sense than anything I was thinking of. I was picturing them all in their coffins waiting for sunset. But I liked his idea better. That they were all out of town except for looters and those people who were locked in the school that night.

The dealership appeared to be empty. There were several four-door Jeeps, and a couple of trucks with extended cabs. I saw a diesel that I would have loved to have a few years ago, but it made too much noise. I kinda wanted something quiet.

There was nothing of value in the car. We had brought the gas cans and planned on finding keys, filling up with the cans, and heading out as quickly as possible.

The door to the dealership was locked, and so were the side doors by the garages. I preferred to go in through the front. It was all glass so and we'd be able to see if anything was coming. Everyone was in the vehicle and Jenny at the wheel. I ran over to the door, knocked on it several times, and then used the tire iron from the truck and hit the glass door.

Okay, yes, I've never broken in before and the tire iron came back and almost knocked me out. As it was, it made me shake my head a few times and when I looked back at the car everyone was trying not to laugh. Well, everyone except Jenny, who had her hands over her mouth and was laughing hard.

Taking a second attempt I pushed the edge of the tire iron between the door and the frame and leaned on it as hard as I could. I pushed until I heard a crack. I did this at a few more spots and hit the glass. This time it shattered.

Looking back, I expected to see applause, but I was met with phony golf claps. I had the revolver and waited. Looking around and expecting someone or something to come out at any moment, but nothing happened. *Wow, what a boring zombie apoca-*

lypse. I could hardly believe I'd just thought that as I stepped through the broken door.

Jenny and Wesley followed. Richard stayed in the car. He had instructions to sound the horn and then either run inside to join us or start the car and get the hell out, depending on what was going on.

He had his slingshot and would not accept another weapon. After seeing him kill a few more rabbits, I didn't doubt his aim. But I worried that they would have to be close to get a good shot in.

"At least it's quiet," he said when we talked about it.

None of us had ever worked for a car dealership, so it took us a while to find the key box, and after prying it open, we found keys that might have worked for the more promising trucks.

We went back to the showroom and pressed the keys, waiting to hear that familiar beep that cars emit to let you know the vehicle was unlocked.

We found a truck that responded to one of the keys. Richard ran to the truck, started it, and pulled it beside the 4x4 four door short bed. I wasn't sure if it was called a crew cab. It didn't matter. The truck had real doors. You know the ones. Not the type that will only open at the back if the ones at the front are already open.

Best of all, it had a locking top for the bed, a black metal panel that you folded up or down and locked your stuff in. It might have come in handy and at least kept shit from falling out if we went cross-country.

We emptied both gas cans into it, which filled a quarter of the tank, and threw the cans in the back.

Our grand theft auto took a total of thirty minutes. Not too bad for first timers. Jenny remembered that the library was between a barbershop and a thrift store.

I made a joke about not wanting to wear last year's fashions. That really wasn't that funny.

There were more cars in front of the library than I had

expected. They were parked on the street and in the adjacent parking lot and a second space beyond.

"Maybe they used this as a loading zone for people when they evacuated?" Wesley wondered.

The library's door wasn't locked. A sign read, 'Coffee inside, buses every hour.' That made no sense to me, but it made me realize that the town might have been empty.

Thank goodness, they still had paper card catalogs. We had made a list of the types of books we needed. I had backed the truck up to the door.

"Four Wheel Drive!" I said in old Tim the Toolman's voice and Richard added, "More Power!"

I looked at the kid in surprise and he said, "Netflix."

We found the card catalog, along with coffee and stale doughnuts. We did a quick run-through, Wesley and I, leaving Jenny and Richard in the front, to make sure we were alone.

I ran more than I'd ever done. There was no one and nothing in the aisles. We checked the front and back sides. Unless someone or something was hiding on top of the shelves, the aisles were safe.

Richard and Jenny took a cart each and started moving down the aisles. Richard was a bookworm, so he was in charge of finding classics along with the technical books we needed. Reading the same sales flier and the same old cereal box for breakfast every day had gotten boring anyway.

They were making good progress and we took one load out to the truck, went back for the second. We grabbed a bunch of fun books, just something to read. I had really enjoyed the Keep in the Light series by David Musser. I had them get all four books. *Guess he never wrote a fifth one,* I thought, and hoped that he was still writing somewhere.

We finished and were about to leave when we heard a noise. I know, I know. You heard a noise, you left, but this sounded like someone yelling for help.

We traced the sound to a back hall that we hadn't checked

out. There was a single door at the far end of the hall. A sign read, 'Emergency Shelter'. The letters were old and faded.

I told everyone I'd heard of places like this, left over from the '50s and '60s. I had actually worked in one that had been converted to hold desks and computers. I didn't want everyone to fall all over themselves on the stairs, so they all stayed in the hall. Richard was closest to the door, with one set of keys to the truck. It was auto-start and lock, so the key just needed to be close to the vehicle to work. I figured Richard and Jenny could get in and, depending on how fast we had to exit, she could drive.

I opened the door.

Nothing jumped at me. I saw stairs leading downwards as I'd expected.

It was dark, so I turned on a flashlight we had found on one of our trips. Not super bright but I'd figured in a pinch it could knock the hell out of something. At the bottom I heard the long, drawn out "Hellllllp!" again. The door had a simple crank lock. There was probably one on the inside as well.

I called out, but I guessed that whoever was inside couldn't hear me.

Twisting the mechanism, the large iron door, similar to one found in a bank vault, slowly slid open. I saw what used to be several people. A man sat, in a cage in the center of the room. Perhaps the cage had once served to protect old books. The man looked like he had once been very fat, but he had lost a lot of weight. I saw several empty containers of water, military rations and a bucket in the cage. The room was lit with a lantern similar to the one we had. At least five zombies shambled around the cage. All of them were looking at me. Then the smell hit me. I'll ever forget that smell.

"Thank God!" he yelled and that distracted them for a second. I shot the first one before it could move and hit it in the shoulder. Then I took my time and shot it in the head, and it dropped. The others were coming for the door. They were moving slowly, but with purpose. Taking my time, I dropped another. I couldn't hear what the guy was yelling, and he was frantically pointing at me.

I fired and put another one down. That left two more, but then I figured out what he was pointing at. I felt a vice grip close on the flashlight arm, saw the mouth heading toward my hand as I shot. I felt the bullet go between my fingers and the zombie dropped, but it didn't let go. I pulled and pulled but I couldn't get free, so I started backing up, dragging the zombie with me. The other two shambled forward, moving slowly with their mouths making that same chewing gesture and their tongues swirling around as I'd observed before. I couldn't hear them or anything right now, but it made me sick imagining them and the smell of the wonderful books was gone. I just smelled filth and shit.

I shot again and dropped one more. Thank goodness they weren't fast. When I fired again and heard the click of hitting an already fired round, my stomach dropped to my feet. I tried to reach in my pocket for extra rounds, but the hand was still holding me, and now that I had reached the bottom step we were stuck.

I felt another hand on me from behind and I thought of Pam. I know people think about different things when they're going to die. I thought of my wife.

Wesley hadn't followed directions. We'd agreed that if he were to hear more than one shot, he was to run like hell and leave me to become zombie food.

But he charged into the action and pulled me backward and shot the last one. Then looking down, he shot the one at my feet. Evidently, I hadn't managed a perfect shot between the fingers of my hand. *Thankfully I still had all my fingers. Especially the nose-picking one,* I thought as I pushed the zombie off. It let go after Wesley had shot it, something I had to file away for later reference.

I reloaded, and while neither of us could hear, he understood that I wanted him to go back up and outside to make sure everyone up there was safe, and to tell the others that this area was secure now, and I would be right up.

I didn't mention the guy in the room and if Wesley had heard him call for help, he never let on.

Taking the flashlight from where I'd dropped it, I did a quick double-take as I entered the room to make sure nothing else was hiding behind the walls.

The man was talking, but I gave him the universal 'Shhh' gesture with my finger, then pointed to my ears and I proceeded to do some breathing and other things I heard would help to get the ringing out. It took a little bit, but eventually I could hear again.

He looked at me, expecting me to open the door, but I wanted to know why he was in here first.

He was trying to unlock the door. I pointed my revolver at him. I couldn't resist quoting from a classic western, "Not so fast, mister." I didn't know whether he got the reference, but he stopped.

He was still a good thirty or so pounds overweight. He wore a dress shirt, untucked, and blue jeans. I could see his jacket over in the corner, along with a lot of rations. I wasn't sure yet whether I would be calling the others down to grab what we could. The rations didn't look as heavy as what we had been grabbing so far. *Let's see what he has to say*, I thought.

I looked at the dead zombies in the room.

"I didn't see any bite marks on some of them. Wonder why that is?" I looked him in the eyes. I knew the answer, but I wanted him to tell me.

"I, I, I'm not sure," he stuttered.

"How about this? You tell me what happened and, if I believe you, I'll take you with us." He smiled at that, and I continued, "If I don't like what you say, but find you just mildly repulsive, I'll leave you locked in the vault." To that, he shook his head and I continued, "If you're really repulsive, I will shoot you. Please tell me your story."

"Really, come on man, I don't know how to start. Just let me out of this cage. Who the hell do you think you are?"

I looked at him, raised the gun to help his motivation.

"Okay, okay. Don't point the gun at me. I have to go back a little."

CHAPTER 7
THE LIBRARIAN'S STORY

The National Guard had been activated several weeks earlier, and the next thing we knew we had a lot of military people in town telling everyone what to do. They started arranging buses and they passed out rations to people.

The Church at the end of 9th Street at the other end of town was a pickup and drop-off point, so they had rations, along with the high school and the library.

Whatever was going on had only just started and no one knew anything. I couldn't get much out of them as they'd started using the area for storage. Who knew that the National Guard had a list of every place that used to have a bomb shelter?

We used to store some rare prints here. Nothing extremely valuable, but a few of them would have earned a couple of grand at an auction.

One of the soldiers, I'm not sure of his rank, or whether people referred to him by his first or last name, was called 'Stan the man' This guy could get anything, the other soldiers said. He could find anything and he was always in the know.

Anyway, Stan and I were shooting the shit over a bottle of scotch. I liked to have a few drinks just after closing while I straightened the shelves. I enjoyed my work, and there was nothing better than a nice evening with a book and some scotch.

Stan started telling me how bad it was further south. Whatever was happening, it'd started down around Jacksonville and went both ways up and down the coast.

"They believe that certain blood types could be more resistant to what is airborne, but if anyone is bit, or badly scratched, there is a 95% chance that they will turn. Normal death is a thing of the past," he said with a grim expression. He'd aged well beyond his years.

We talked more and more into the night, and he showed me pictures on his cell phone of some of them crawling out of their graves. I didn't know if he was bullshitting me or not, but the clips looked real and not like any movie I had ever seen.

They were finding towns that had very few infected and inventoried everyone. Look, I've got a barcode. Let me pull up my shirt. Right here.

Anyway, after getting personal details from all of us, they started sending in buses. He didn't know where they were shipping people. "It really is a cluster fuck. If I was you, Charlie," he said.

"I'm sorry did I tell you my name? I'm Charlie, the librarian."

He continued, "If I was you, Charlie, I would hole up here. Find some people like you, maybe a girl, and don't take the last bus out."

I started thinking more and more about this as the buses were pulling out. I didn't know if I would have taken the bus or not, but as it was, I didn't get a chance.

"Attention everyone, attention. If you do not have a pass and try to board, you will be shot," they said over different loudspeakers. I had seen a lot of the townspeople get on earlier buses. I'd drawn a high number so I would be on the next to last or last bus.

I volunteered to make coffee and help out distributing food.

We had locked it in the cage to prevent anyone from taking it and I was given a key.

The bus pulled up, and people were getting on in a fairly orderly fashion until the first person screamed. There was a mass of zombies coming up the road. Some were doing that slow shuffle you must have seen, but others moved like fucking track stars.

Stan had told me that as far as they could tell, their speed was related to how they had turned. The ones that had been bitten died slowly and moved slow. The ones that had caught the sickness usually died and turned within twenty-four hours. After that, they moved fast as hell.

Someone screamed. I think it was Martha McGowan, but I'm not sure and the hoard of zombies just started moving that much faster. I could see them running up the street, their tongues doing that circling motion.

Stan said, "Better get below." He took off to catch his ride, "If we can, we will come back for you. Hole up as long as you can."

A few others must have heard him, because they followed me as I moved inside. I had no idea how long it would take for someone to come. I ran down the stairs, taking two and three steps at a time. I got the door open with a couple of people just behind me.

"Fucking asshole", "Where are you going", "The zombies are coming", "Please save my daughter." That last one was the worst things they shouted. A woman tried to shove her baby into my arms.

I couldn't get the outer door shut, but I made the cage. I think that they thought that once they were in the room, they would shut the door and be alright. They didn't expect me to keep running for the cage.

Once inside, I shut the door, locked it, and then started moving everything as far from the edges as I could. I didn't want anyone reaching through.

The zombies followed them down the stairs. Oh wait, there

weren't any dead zombies on the stairs. That was the funniest thing. They carried the bodies away. Stan said that scientists at NASA had reported that they behaved like bees or ants. It was called necrophoresis.

He'd told me that he'd been in places that had held twenty or thirty dead. When he'd gone back the next day to burn them, they had gone. No one was sure where they are taking them, but it was fucking creepy.

They were too worried about the zombies on the stairs to worry about me. I noticed that the baby and woman had been crushed against the back wall as more and more people tried to get in here. Right over there.

Those behind me shut the door. In a last 'Oh fuck you' moment, those left outside hit the latch that prevented our lock from turning.

The door was a terrible design for a bomb shelter, but what did I know? It was the first bomb shelter I'd ever been locked in.

We heard screaming and that shuffling sound and then everything went quiet. That was when they noticed me. I didn't like being in the dark, so I had turned on one of the crank radio lights that was stored down here.

They all came at the cage in an instant. They tried to reach their arms through it. They tried to get the food or to me. Some were throwing stuff at me. A few tried to use their clothes to hook something.

"Calm down people," I said, "There is plenty of food here, and plenty of water. Just relax, and I will distribute it."

I did. I started passing out food to them, I told them that I didn't know how long this would go and that I wanted to make sure everyone had food.

It worked fairly well for the first twenty-four hours. But when people had to go to the bathroom things got messy. We could still hear the zombies outside. We had bags for it, but have you ever tried to shit in a bag? Anyway, not the most fun I've ever had.

I told them, well, in fact, I lied to them that the National Guard would be coming back and that they would come looking for us. I figured this was unlikely to happen, but since they had seen that Stan and I were close, maybe he would come back.

On the third day, tempers started to flair again. "Who put you in charge?", "I'm going to ruin you when this is over!" They said worse things. One of the women started whispering to me at night about how good she was going to be to me. I unzipped my pants, and she was stroking me gently at first, but then the bitch grabbed me and tried to pull me closer to the bars by my cock, so that her man could get hold of me.

It was close for a while, but I got away from them, and I punished them. "No food for anyone for twelve hours," I told them. The next time they tried something similar a few days later, I cut their food and water for twenty-four hours.

It was hard watching them all get weaker, but I wanted to stay strong, so at some point, I could open the door and see about the lock. Maybe I could use my toolbox to take it apart and open it from the inside.

Yes, yes, I had a toolbox, right under here. I would have given it to them, but they would have taken the cage apart.

Let's see, I think we were on day eight or ten when some of the men started fighting. I told them to stop, threw my bag of shit at them, and really, I just wanted things to be quiet. You have to remember, I'm a reader, so being locked in with all of these books, I just needed quiet, and I would have been happy.

I had a first edition of Salem's Lot. I knew nothing of Shakespeare. For me, Salem's Lot was wonderful word porn. I hadn't read it in a while and I was looking forward to it.

Fuckhead 1 hit fuckhead 2 and said that his wife had stolen a candy bar, and they started fighting. Then the wife's shirt got ripped off. I'm a guy and it had been a long time and even as she kept her bra on, I was well excited. I wasn't paying much attention to what was going on. Next thing I knew, a makeshift rope was thrown over my head from behind. Only one of them was back there. He pulled me so hard backward that I hit my head on the cage. I was lucky I tripped, or he would have pulled me right to the bars. They'd made the rope out of some old signs that'd been hanging up. They'd told me that they were cutting fabric for toilet paper.

I turned off the lights. I have two of those crank lights, and I had kept them on for everyone's benefit, but now they'd done this to me. I plunged us all into darkness, and from then on, I only turned the light on when I had to go, or when they threw shit or something else my way.

There wasn't anything too hard outside the cage, and I had built myself a little bed and supply fort to lay down in. Laying in there kept the smell down some.

What… Did I have a plan? No, not really. I guess if I did have a plan, it was to let them get weaker until I could get out of the cage and work on the lock. I was even thinking of switching places with them, but do you know how long it takes for people to get weak from starvation or lack of water? Well, I didn't know. Turned out it took about three days until some started to pass out.

I noticed this, and the fact that their pleas had gotten weaker.

My plan would have worked if fuckhead 1 hadn't taken pity on his wife. I heard something new, a sucking sound, and I quickly turned on the light. Her tongue was going around and around, and she was very fast. She'd been the one by the door. Anyway, she was eating her husband's arm, and the last thing he said was, "I only did it to help you find peace."

The rest you know. Hey, what are you doing? Where are you going? Come back here. Come back here. You can't leave me in here. I will get out. I have my tools. I'll come find you!

You can't leave meeeee!

CHAPTER 8
OUT OF DODGE

His voice rang in my ears as I stood beside the closed door. "You can't leave meeeee!"

I was sure that he'd told his story putting as much sugar on it as possible, so it may have happened like that. But I didn't see any open food containers outside of the cage that hadn't been emptied before they'd been tossed.

I had already decided not to tell the others about locking him in. I would say that he was scared and wanted to wait for the bus. If any wanted to wait with him, I'd discourage it. I doubted they would.

When I shut the door, I saw the latch he'd been talking about that had been fixed so it wouldn't open from the inside. Bending down I took the shoelaces from one of the zombies' feet. Stan's story about them carrying off their dead was creepy as hell. I guess they could only do that if the door was open or could be pushed in, since the zombie in the gas station was still there. Anyway, shoeless here would have to be barefoot for his trip. I tied the laces to the latch. Even if the librarian was able to get his tools working to get to the mechanism to move the latch, it would stay in place.

He was getting air from someplace, most likely filtered, and had plenty of food and water. A prison of his own making, I thought it was fitting.

"Is he coming?" Jenny asked, and I shook my head, "He wants to wait for the bus. I told him where we were in case he decided to join us."

"I think we should try going cross-country. Maybe not today, but spending time in the mountains is not a bad play. We should stop at that camping store we saw," I said as we all climbed into the truck.

Everything worked out well for another couple of weeks. We were happy in the cabin. There was no other news over the radio, and Wesley and Richard even decided to move back into their cabin. It was a little down the hill, but close enough to hear shots if they hit trouble. They also knew about the truck that we had stashed and our slide for life. If anything happened, that was where we would meet up.

On the morning of the last day in the cabin, I woke early and bent over the toilet to spit in it. It was a habit I'd picked up from my old man. I noticed a little blood. Not much, but to be expected. I sort of lost track of time but thought that it had been about four months since the world had stopped.

The FM stations were all offline, and the AM ones broadcast every now and then. One station had a young radio host. He had been an intern for a sports show and had lucked out since the hosts had decided to stay home on Z-Day.

He had food and water to sustain himself. It took him three days of good sunlight to broadcast for a half-hour in the morning and evening. Listeners were to expect downtime if a big storm came through.

"I'm trying my best to stay on the air. If anyone has any news of any safe zones, please make your way there," he said and gave an address. He added, "I have a CB radio on channel 18.

That used to be the trucker channel when I was a kid, but unfortunately, I don't hear anything on it."

It was very sad, hearing this lone voice on the air. He would talk about his life and provide all the news that he had from the wire. I wasn't sure what he was talking about, something that would go to radio stations before everything went off the air.

I really enjoyed his talk about celebrity gossip that had happened months earlier. He must have gone through the entire radio station grabbing every magazine he could find, and he treated everything as if it were current news.

"You will never guess who was seen this weekend with a pop icon..." or "They sold their mansion for fifteen million dollars and are now moving to Florida."

We knew it wasn't current, or even real, since that world was gone. But it did give us something else to think of for those couple weeks. He would even tease us with a "Tune in tomorrow to find out who was caught with...".

I was checking out maps and tried to come up with a plan that would let Jenny get to safety. I figured that whenever things went to crap where we were, we would head up north, back to my house to pick up some more weapons and food stocks.

Yes, yes, I had long been a 'world ending in 2012' kind of person. The Mayans only missed it by a few years. And since some of the food stocks I had said 'good for twenty', I hadn't been the only one thinking about it.

We had the camping gear, and if my plan to drive along the powerlines worked, we could make it around some of the roadblocks we'd heard about.

Jenny came into the bathroom looking sleepy-eyed. "You know, I'd kill for hot water," she said. She kissed me and got into the shower.

"Come join me."

I did, taking time to brush my teeth before kissing her deeply. It was cold, but we kept each other warm.

Later, we both dressed. We even put our shoes on. I had told everyone that unless they were in the shower or sleeping to keep their shoes on as well. I know it made no sense since we had spent several months in peace, but I just figured it would happen right about the time I had mine off and then I'd be running through that tower with my bare feet. "Like Die Hard," I said. And can you believe it? Jenny had never seen the movie, so my reference was useless.

If my generator was still working, I thought we might watch that before heading out of the house. It would be nice to watch a few minutes of television or a movie again.

I heard the gunshots,. At first thought I thought they were just thunder. "Get ready and keep an eye out. Things go bad, hit the slide and we will meet at the truck or the diner," I said running out of the cabin. I had the revolver in a makeshift holster, and a deer rifle I had found, with the scope, so this was my best weapon until I could get to whoever was coming. For that I had a wonderful double-barrel shotgun loaded with double-aught buckshot. Figure to use it as a club while reloading.

Jenny had her a small lever action. I left our stolen truck parked behind the cabin and ran down the hill toward Wesley's and Richard's cabin.

When I got close, I saw both of them firing from different windows, and it sounded like they were moving between the front windows and the ones I saw them shooting from. *Making more noise for me*, I thought.

It took me a few seconds before I saw them. They were so covered in mud, dirt, and leaves that they blended into the landscape. Most were the slow-moving kind, and once I saw them, I could pick them out.

It was like one of those posters that were popular when I was a kid. Can you see the spider?

Anyway, you know the ones. I found a good spot and concentrated on the ones between me and the cabin. This was something we had discussed before. Whether it was us or them who were under attack, the plan was to clear the way.

I fired, used the bolt to load a new shell, and fired again a few seconds later. The shots were spot on. Headshots both. I had always been a decent shot, as you know, but give me a good scope and a rest and I can put two lines on where I want the shell to go.

I kept firing at different ones, not bothering to count them. There must have been more than a dozen.

One of them turned its head, sniffed in the air and looked straight at me. "Fuck," I said as it started to run up the hill. I remembered all that I'd said about putting the lines where I wanted them. Well, that was easy when the target was slow. The one charging me now was more difficult to take down.

I missed once when it stepped in a ditch on the way up. My shot went over its head. I took a deep breath. Looked down the hill to assume where it would go and planned my shot. I put the crosshairs about five feet in front of it and as soon as I saw something in the scope I shot. The first shot hit it in the chest, driving it back. Fifty yards being shot with a .308 would have hurt like a mother if it could have felt anything. I bet it was like being hit with a sledgehammer.

It stopped and before it could run again, I fired. This time, my aim was true.

There were a lot more of them around the cabin. Wesley and Richard made a break for it and I covered them. I was shooting and reloading as fast as I could when they ran past me, yelling, "They came from everywhere at once!"

I didn't like the sound of that. I put the rifle over my shoulder and grabbed the shotgun and took off after them. All of us were loaded down with what we considered essential, which was mostly guns.

Jenny was outside our cabin, keeping watch. I guessed that when she heard the shots, she figured it was time to get the hell out of Dodge.

"Get to the beach," I yelled, and she waved and ran around the back of the cabin. I hated to leave the new truck, but I noticed a lot of them on the road. It almost seemed like a herd of them. *Could that be possible?*

I almost died then. One of them had been standing behind a tree. I swear it let Wesley and Richard go by. If Richard hadn't looked back to see where I was at that very moment, I'd have been dead.

"Tree!" he shouted, pointing, and almost fell down himself, but his dad grabbed him.

I turned and let loose both barrels as it leapt out at me. I am not kidding. Fucking jumping zombies. Anyway, that took care of it, and I reloaded as I kept walking. If I had been thinking more, I'd have noticed how wet his clothes were. Maybe that would have saved…

Looking up as I rounded the cabin, Jenny was already flying down the slide for life. Laughing. I swear the girl was laughing. Yes, way too young for me, and wearing a cartoon character backpack she'd found.

She looked back and I waved. I was still not putting two and two together on the wet zombie.

Richard and Wesley grabbed the hooks of the zip line. Jenny had laid out all our backpacks. I put mine on, keeping an eye out and I gave them a few seconds to get going. No need to jam things up and who knew how much weight the line can handle.

I jumped on as Jenny went over the last hill and out of sight, and it was then that I thought about the wet zombies. Too late.

I couldn't make the line go any faster. I knew there was danger ahead of me, and I heard the gunshots before I saw anything. I was still twenty feet up going fast. I was too high to jump.

Coming out of the trees, I saw the three of them on the beach, Richard and Wesley taking the boat to the water, and Jenny standing there with her lever-action rifle, shooting from a standing position. She looked like Annie Oakley, her hair flying every which way as she fired.

Since the slide on the zip line required me to keep both hands on it, I couldn't draw and shoot. I was at fate's mercy.

The zombies were coming out of the water. They were coming from opposite side of the lake from where our truck was hidden. It looked like there were thousands of them. All the ones from the school and more, and while that was odd enough, they were all shuffling along in some type of order. They were forming a wedge pattern, its point moving toward Jenny. The ones that had entered the water kept walking as it got deeper. They just keep walking, their bodies sinking lower and lower, until they had completely submerged.

I could picture them shuffling along the bottom of the lake in that same slow march.

As I reached the end of the line, I yelled, "They're in the water."

But no one heard me over Jenny's shots. When she saw me, she started running for the boat, just as we'd agreed. All three now pushed the boat out further.

I ran as fast as I could, yelling, and made it to the boat, but I was too late. Wesley was being pulled under. I heard his gun go off several times underwater and he was back on top. Pushing the boat further into the lake.

"Get in!" he yelled at me, and I saw the sadness in his eyes.

"I'm sorry," I said, and our eyes met. We should have spent days talking about how he wanted me to take care of his son, and him knowing I would do this, and all of that passed through our connection. He shoved the boat forward.

Richard screamed, "NOOOOOOOO!", and I held onto him, to keep him from tipping the boat. We were too far and deep for the zombies could reach out, but if one of us fell in….

"He got bit. He saved us!" I yelled, and Richard got very still as he watched his father turn around. Wesley had dropped the gun and had his machete slashing and chopping at the unseen ones in the water. He was standing his ground, protecting his son, and us.

"Live well!" he yelled back over his shoulder and his son responded, "I love you, daddy." I started paddling. The entire herd was now moving toward us. I noticed more of them onshore with their noses cocked in the air, sniffing.

Fuck me, I thought, *God damned birdlike zombies.*

We made it to shore and dropped our backpacks in the bed of the truck. We slammed Jenny's and my rifle into the gun rack. Richard held on to his weapon. His slingshot was in his pocket. We hopped in the truck. Richard sat on the passenger side, with Jenny in the middle. Richard wrapped his arms around her and cried. I started driving.

I didn't say anything. Jenny did a lot of talking and at one point reached up and took my hand in hers. I knew she was crying and worried for all of us, but right then she comforted that boy better than I ever could.

Later, as we continued down the road, he said, "He took out a bunch of those sons of bitches, didn't he?"

CHAPTER 9
CONFESSION

I was surprised by how empty the roads were. Yes, there were cars blocking the way at times, but we were able to get around most of them without too much trouble, thanks to the truck's 4x4 system. I decided to take 81 as far north as I could. I would get off on 66 and head towards Front Royal and 522, so that I could make it home.

We had to stop a few times to push cars off the road, but we didn't see any zombies or people. It was eerily quiet.

"You notice there are no military vehicles?" Jenny asked.

Looking around as I pushed a small VW out of the way, I scratched my head trying to think where we had most recently seen a military vehicle.

We passed several police cruisers but we didn't see any police or anyone else who might have helped us. I spent a little time pulling the radio out of one the cruisers. I figured if there was time, I would wire it into the truck when we get to my place.

Richard had stopped talking. He held Jenny's hand. No matter what we said, he wouldn't come out of it.

We took Route 66 exit for Front Royal. I said, more to Jenny than Richard, "Did you know this was once called Hell Town?" She didn't and I continued, "That was the late 1700s or early

1800s. It earned that nickname thanks to all the livestock wranglers and boatmen on the Shenandoah River, who would visit the local saloons."

I know, I told you more of this story before, but it was the first time Jenny ever heard it. Richard perked up and said, "After this is all over, if there are any humans left, I bet it starts out like those early days."

He was right, and it was good to have him talking again. We started naming historical periods we wanted to have back. We settled on kings, and knights and beautiful maidens.

"So, you want me to call you my king now?" Jenny asked and when I nodded my head, she hit me in the arm and we all laughed.

It was good for me. My hope was we could hole up in the house for a bit. I had some plywood that I could put on the windows. We had the two-car garage and enough trees around to keep us warm when the propane tanks were empty.

I'd worked on a generator tied to the creek but the only thing it could power was a few outdoor lights, but that would be good for a little while. I really wanted to run the big generator, but it was too noisy. With these things being like birds of sorts, I didn't want to give them anything to latch onto.

Once we hit 522, I knew I was home. I could have run blindfolded through the woods, and I'd have got them there.

Pulling up to the gate, I was happy to see that it was still shut. This used to be a farm with cattle, and not only did it have the cattle gate in the ground, but it also had a gate with a chain across. I'd planned to be gone for a while, so I'd locked it on the way out. The fact that the lock was intact made me feel good.

Living at the end of a long lane came in handy, especially now. Unless someone was sure which turn-off was mine, they would have to be right behind me to follow me home.

When I got back into the truck after opening the gate, Jenny asked, "Don't you want to get your mail?"

I remembered we had agreed I would call when we got to the hotel or to our first stop, to put a hold on mail.

"I think civilization kept going a few more days here than it did where we've just come from, but no, leave it in there. If someone comes by, they won't notice we've been here."

After I pulled through, I got out and shut the gate again. I made sure to put the chain back exactly the way I remembered it. In principle, I trusted most of my neighbors. But since the rebirth of society, I didn't trust anyone that much anymore.

The house was as I had left it. I got my spare key, went through, and manually opened the garage and we pulled in. I shut the garage and we all let out a collective breath we didn't know we'd been holding.

I turned the water on. I had a well - fresh water for at least a hundred years, the guy who'd drilled it had said. I wanted try to run the outside lights in. Maybe we could get the TV going in the basement. I had a lot of DVDs.

After showing Jenny and Richard around, we decided to split up and get to work. Jenny and Richard were to move the mattresses down to the basement. It would be good to sleep on a mattress again, but until we'd made sure that no light escaped the house, we planned to live in the basement at night.

My cordless drill was still charged. Happy, I grabbed some plywood and did my best to seal off all the windows. I did this from the inside. I know, not as good as doing it from the outside, but I didn't want to be outside any more than I had to. Those things could smell me. And I didn't want anyone walking by to see that something had changed.

The house was solid, and the windows were solid so while someone or something could eventually get in, they would make a hell of a lot of noise trying.

Jenny boiled water upstairs but she didn't drop any of the rations we had into the water until she was in the basement with the door shut. I even went so far as to duct tape the door. "No need to chance the smell getting out. I'm too paranoid, I know,"

Richard interrupted, adding, "I don't think dad and I were paranoid enough."

He broke down again. We all sat and ate in silence, and dammit, I wanted one more night. I wanted one more night of happiness with this girl, but I was spitting blood every time I bent over from the pain. When I took a shit, there was blood in that as well.

I asked Jenny if she remembered how pissed off I'd been when she'd first met me. She laughed and told Richard about our first meeting, and her ex, and how I came running like some type of hero. "My hero," she called me then, and I felt so bad I couldn't tell her, but I had to.

I knew that she planned to go as far as she could with me and be safe. We had talked about a boat, and other things that may have been possible near the river, but while I was helping with the ideas, I told her I didn't want to plan too far ahead.

"Let's get back home first, and then decide."

I held her hand, and just like ripping off a band-aid, I told her. I told her I estimated that I had about six months left, maybe a little more or less.

"What medicine do you need?" she asked, and I told her that even with medical treatment I could only hope for a very painful three or four more months.

It was one of the hardest conversations I've ever had. She hit me on the chest several times demanding, "Why did you let me love you?" To that, I had no answer except the truth.

"Because I'm selfish and I didn't want to die alone."

Richard started crying, probably thinking about his dad. Jenny went into the bathroom for a bit.

Yes, you are right. I just sat there. I've never known what to do when women are unhappy and it was my fault. If I can't buy ice cream to fix it, I'm not much good.

Richard and I cleaned up. I went outside and ran an extension cord just to be doing something. I wasn't too bothered about watching anything

I unplugged the TV from the wall socket and plugged it into the extension cord. The power from the creek went to a set of batteries, and some other things my brother-in-law had helped me rig years earlier when I'd been thinking about going off the grid, but the only thing I'd ever powered off the batteries were the outside lights.

Before I tried the power, Jenny came out. She wrapped her arms around my neck and kissed me. Then standing there, she hugged me, saying, "I'm sorry. I was being stupid. Forgive me?"

"There is nothing to forgive. If the world hadn't ended, who knows what would have happened. As it is, I've loved you more than I had a right to. Thank you," I told her and kissed her. Richard was getting uncomfortable, so I said. "Let's give this a try."

Pressing the power button, nothing happened. "Shit," I said aloud, and then I pressed it again. This time I started laughing like a mad man. "Wait here," I demanded and took off upstairs.

I'm sure they heard me rummaging through my cabinets to find the last two double-A batteries on the planet. Well, the last two I had. I put them in the remote, handed it to Richard, and said, "You try."

He did and it came on.

"I'm sure not there's enough to power the satellite up there, but before we leave here, I can turn the generator on and we can channel surf to see if anything is being broadcast. The TV has a built-in DVD player on the side."

"DVD?" they both looked at me questioningly, then started laughing. Jenny added, "Did you get them at a video store? I heard back in olden times that is what they did."

Jenny sat with me on the couch. Richard sat in my chair pushing it way back. We started watching my favorite Christmas movie. *Die Hard*. They both enjoyed it and I went to find some chips in the pantry.

"I'd try to make popcorn, but I don't know how much power

we have for the microwave. Maybe tomorrow we try, with the TV off."

We went to bed early and all slept better than we had in a while. Earlier in the evening, I had taken the drill and screwed a few boards across the basement steps. Sure, we were locked in, but having an ax and a ladder in the back room, I could always go through the floor if we had to. *Maybe tomorrow I will make a trap door. Be good to have more than one way out.*

The next couple of weeks gave us a little bit of paradise. I felt very sorry for Richard, but I was amazed at how strong he was and how hard he worked.

Since they both knew what was going to happen to me, I started training them on every gun we had. If I didn't know how to load or work them, I would figure it out and show them.

Richard started holding school for all of us with those books his dad had, and we started trying to figure out where to go next.

Late one night after Jenny had gone to sleep, Richard came to me and said, "Do you think we could make it to Pennsylvania?"

"The roads have been clear so far, so I'm not sure, but I would guess we can. Why? Family?" I asked and he nodded.

"Mom's side. Dad and I didn't go back too much after she'd passed. We went back for family dinners and reunions. Enough to stay connected, but it made him so sad, I stopped asking to go." He was crying, ashamed at his confession.

"We all do what we must when it comes to our parents and loved ones. Yes, we should go to PA. Do you think there is a good place for them to survive?" I asked and he went on describing the farm they lived on, the mountains, the streams, and all the wildlife. "Sounds perfect."

After talking to Jenny about it in the morning, I turned on the generator. It would likely snow in a few weeks I wanted to get going so that we could come back if they were not there or make a different plan depending on whether there was anything on the satellite.

There wasn't. Several emergency messages were edited into a loop, but there wasn't any original programming.

"Shame you don't have a… what did you call it, a ham radio?" Richard said as I turned off the power to the generator.

Laughing, I said, "I may know where to find one. Let's visit Don."

CHAPTER 10
HOARDER

My friend Don was a hoarder. There was no good way to think of him as anything else. Since I've known him, I have had to personally help him brace his floor twice because of the weight of all the newspapers he kept. He wasn't rich by any means, but he spent his money on newspapers, magazines, books, and his ham radio setup.

He'd taught me just enough to turn it on, with the help of the books he had, but perhaps we would luck out and find him alive.

We decided to pack everything we needed, just in case we didn't make it back. Richard helped me load the generator onto the truck. I packed a couple of extension cords. If Don didn't have a generator hookup on the outside of his house, I could make one, using the old suicide plugs, the ones with two male connectors. If one wasn't careful, these were perfectly capable of frying a person.

Don didn't live far. As we pulled into his driveway, I saw his windmill turning. When I'd been working on my small light setup, he'd been putting in a windmill and some solar panels. *Be interesting to see what he got going.*

He lived in the middle of about fifty acres of woods so I felt fairly confident no one else would hear when I yelled up to the house from the gate. "Don, it's Nick! You home?"

Even without the zombies running around, I would have called from his gate like this. He did the same at my house. We weren't used to neighbors from other parts of the country walking up to your porches to knock on the door.

I yelled again, "Don, it's Nick!"

"Who's with you?" I heard him yell back, seeing a little bit of an upstairs curtain move.

"Jenny and Richard, they're friends and good. Not sick. We have food if you need it. Wanted to check on the radio."

"Food, well why didn't you say so? Head on up!" he yelled over his shoulder, and I knew he was heading down to unlock the door.

Opening the gate, we all moved inside. I noticed the tape on the inside of the doors. Don, shaking my hand, said, "They smell…" and we both finished together, "…like birds."

"Have they been here?" I asked.

"No, did you hear about that?"

We were all in the living room. Jenny and Richard marveled at the stacks of magazines.

"No, Don, we saw it. I swear they were moving as birds do in a wedge shape. Fucking things walked right into a lake and kept going until they reached the other side."

Don shook his head and motioned us to come into the kitchen. Jenny put a small cooler on the table and started unpacking the food. We had some stuff that would go bad on the road and figured we might as well have a feast at Don's.

"Anything on the radio?"

He shook his head, smiled and motioned me upstairs. I told Richard to stay with Jenny. Upstairs, Don whispered, "They, okay?"

I smiled and filled him in all that we had gone through. I told him that they weren't part of a government conspiracy. There was no alien DNA. We discussed a couple of other conspiracy theories we had debated over the years. It was fun to talk, and before going into what he had heard on the ham radio, he said, "Moon landing's still fake. I don't care what you say, even after Shatner went up. Now, look here…" And he showed me a bunch of maps, he'd been keeping track of.

"Originally, we had ten safe zones near-by. Luray Caverns, Shenandoah Caverns, and others. They thought that if people could gather in these locations, there'd be plenty of water, and there'd be food was nearby." He moved a couple of papers and continued.

"Most of these places fell quickly. People already bit got in, thinking that they were immune. One of these places had a god damned graveyard in it. I had heard rumors about it for years that someone was buried in the Shenandoah Caverns, but I had no proof. Well, now we know."

I must have had an odd look on my face because he stopped.

"You mean you haven't heard? Damn Nick, where have you been? Things we know. They infect living people when they bite them. The recently dead come back to life fairly quickly, in a matter of days. But what was really crazy was that they came out of graves from fifty years ago, right out of the ground."

He showed me a couple of emails, and printouts of some websites that had been active after things had gone strange. Don had cable internet and satellite and the latter must have stayed up for a while.

"Anyone buried in modern times is still down there. Most are now put in concrete vaults. Most are likely trying to get out."

"Pam!"

"Oh shit, I'm sorry Nick. I didn't think about Pam. No one knows whether the vaults are sealed. Okay, I don't know about them for sure."

"It's okay. You told me that most of the safe zones fell. Any still going up and running?" I asked, changing the subject.

Don moved over to his workbench. He limped a little and we both said, "Gout."

He laughed and said, "Damn stuff hits me when it rains, or when the sun is shining. This time, I just bumped my leg on a chair. That's why I'm limping around. Look here, Nick," he said pointing to another map. "A hospital ship called Mercy lies just off the coast. I get a signal from them every day. It's always on the same band, and it's not a recording. They say they have food and supplies and anyone who gets to the ship will be taken to an island that has been cleansed. They're not saying which island, which I kinda understand."

"Cleansed is an odd word, don't you think?" I asked.

He had no response, looked at his watch, and said, "They are broadcasting again in a few hours. I think we should contact them and let them know that there are three on the way."

"What do you mean three? Aren't you coming?" I asked

And to that, he waved his arms wide and said, "I've worked for this my entire life. I can't leave."

I went into research mode, looking at everything he had. There were references to food stockpiles. While things had gone from bad to worse very quickly, most people were not in the Mad Max zone. Most people were helping others. Yes, there were a few assholes, but they'd been assholes when the world had still been 'normal'.

When we went down to eat, Don let me have a few of the maps.

Jenny and Richard liked the idea of the hospital ship, but Richard wanted to check on his family first. We agreed that we would swing up that way to Pennsylvania, check on his family. If the situation was solid, we'd stay there. If not, we'd head to the ocean.

I couldn't convince Don to come with us.

After we'd eaten, we went up to see if the hospital ship reached out. Don had an idea. He put forth some calls to different ham radio operators on the east coast. We were trying to find anyone had knowledge of the county where Richard's kin were. We didn't want to broadcast the names, unless we found someone from the area.

It took a while, but we got in touch with someone who called himself the sheriff of Franklin County.

"The Old Stockwell farm, is that the one?" he asked over the radio.

Looking at Richard who nodded, yes, Don sent back an affirmative.

"I'm sorry, but I haven't heard from anyone there for a few weeks. We will go up in the morning and let you know in the afternoon."

Don thanked the sheriff.

"You know, the sheriff was happy to have something he could do. I'm sure there's been so much happening that was just out of their control. It's a remote farm, so hopefully we'll get good news," I said.

The hospital ship was right on time. It opened with a generic message and then they were live. They were talking numbers, primarily about how many survivors they wanted before taking off for the next trip. They described the boarding process, and made sure to tell listeners not to congregate on the dock before the ship's arrival. "These things have a sense of smell that must rival a bloodhound. We have set up a perimeter with gates, and locks that require basic human intelligence, so please make sure to close them after you come through. If they do show up in large numbers, we will close up and pick up at an alternate area, until they move on."

Don broadcast back to the ship, "We have three souls that need transport."

"That's wonderful news. We will let you know an approximate time to get to the area tomorrow."

They sent some letters and numbers.

When Richard and Jenny looked at me, I said, "Call sign, think of it like an official CB handle," and both looked at me like I was crazy.

Next movie will be Convoy, I thought.

The hospital ship gave us focus and hope. Well, if it was there. I didn't trust anyone, but we would see. We would stake out the pickup location. If it looked safe, we'd go up.

That night, I slept fitfully. My thoughts kept returning to Pam, trying to get out of her coffin. When I woke up, I was coughing. I tried my best not to wake up Jenny as I went into the shower.

Don had hot water. It was wonderful to wash and actually feel clean again. The steam helped my lungs as I took in moist, hot air.

As I came out of the shower, Jenny was there. She helped me dry off and looked up. "You aren't going to go with us on the ship, or stay at Don's, are you?"

I shook my head.

"But the hospital ship could fix you?" she protested.

"Maybe, but I doubt it. Let's see what they say about Richard's family, and then we'll decide."

We made breakfast and sat around reading Don's magazines. He made me pack up a few to take on the road and said to tell the ship that if they needed some, he was happy to lend them out. I think he was kind of proud to own something useful.

I wanted to go and listen for the sheriff with Don, but Richard wouldn't have any of that. As I'd feared, it was bad news. He told us that he'd had to take out several zombies in the area and mentioned that some of them had risen from a family plot.

Richard remembered the plot. We thanked the sheriff and mentioned the hospital ship.

"You tell them where we are and when they find a cure, we'd love to hear about it. But until then, most of us are staying put. My family has been in these hills for hundreds of years and we're not about to run out now."

I gave Don most of our food. We'd come back if something

bad happened. I gave him the generator and some spare gas. We took just enough to get us to the ship and back.

We could always siphon more gas from abandoned cars.

We were all sad about Richard's family. Jenny held him in her arms. She didn't say anything, but I could tell she was hoping that the hospital ship could help me.

Don and I shook hands, simply saying, "C ya," and we headed out.

I did tell him that we'd reach out from the hospital ship if possible, to let him know we'd made it.

CHAPTER 11
BOAT RIDE

We talked a lot about different things on the road. Jenny wanted me to go with them, but I wasn't so sure. I thought about it, but there were things I had to take care of. After what Don had told me, I had to think of Pam. *Could you be in a concrete tomb trying to claw you way out?* The thought of it made me shake.

Jenny touched my hand, leaned closer to me and I put my arm around her. "Nick, I didn't want to say anything, but I'm pregnant. I know that this is not the best time to bring a life into this world, but as they say, life finds a way."

Pulling her close, I kissed the top of her head.

"I love you."

That made the decision. I didn't say it, but I would take the ship with her, and try my best to beat my illness.

Perhaps the hospital ship had things that my doctor, Mr. Ass Hat, didn't know about.

I almost missed it. I saw a car pull out from behind a highway sign as we went by. I wouldn't have thought anything about the sign, but I just happened to look in the rearview mirror as I popped over a hill.

"Jenny, Richard, get ready. We've trouble coming up. I'm not sure from which direction, but they're setting a trap."

I was proud to see both were checking their weapons.

I described the car. I told them that I assumed there'd be an obstacle up ahead that we would not be able to pass. Then, while turning around, the car would ride up.

We were on a two-lane road. It wasn't an interstate and I spotted a driveway that branched off down a hill. I knew that whoever they were, they would be looking down the road, so I pulled in. I had Richard and Jenny both get out. They grabbed their weapons as they exited the truck. Richard ran up to the road to signal me when they were fifty yards away.

Neither of them argued. If they'd had a better idea, they would have mentioned, but this was the best strategy we had.

As soon as I saw the signal, I floored the truck, backing up the hill. If I arrived too late, they'd pass and miss me. If I was too early, I'd park in the center and let them hit me or force them to stop. They would hit the passenger side, I'd be fine.

We'd timed it perfectly. I flew back up the hill and I hit the car broadside. I kept the gas all the way down until I drove them off the road on the opposite side of the road.

I got a few gray hairs when I tried to pull forward in order to avoid going over the bank with them. Luck was on my side.

Richard and Jenny were both running toward the car. So far, no gunshots. I noticed that both airbags were deployed as I got out of the truck.

Jenny was the first to shoot, and Richard quickly followed. It was over quick, and we didn't wait around. "We can backtrack a little and go around. No reason to stay here."

The truck didn't ride very well, but nothing was blocking the tires. The wheels were way out of alignment, but I felt it would make the trip.

Jenny held my hand and said, "Did you see the back seat?" When I shook my head, she kept talking.

"They had zombies in the back. Looked like they were chained up. Who would do something like that?"

I didn't know why and was glad we didn't have to find out. We backtracked and continued on our way.

Jenny and Richard slept as I drove the final stretch. They were resting up in case things were bad when we got there. I kept my eyes on the rearview mirror, but nothing was following us.

Towards sunrise, I could smell salt in the air. I held Jenny's hand, wishing we were on a nice ride to the beach.

I found a spot where we could watch the pier and have an escape route. Using Don's binoculars, I spotted the ship on the edge of the horizon. They'd told Don that they would move toward this dock today, to another one tomorrow, and finally to a third and last one on Friday.

I saw a couple of people in other buildings, and in their cars. Everyone stayed away from the pier. The ship's captain had told anyone listening to stay away until the ship was almost to the dock. Everyone was to board as quickly as possible before they came out of the sand, from under the boardwalk or the dock.

The ship would blow its air horn once when the doors were opening and we'd have ten minutes to make it into the hold. If zombies had managed to get in with us, it was our responsibility to deal with them. They wouldn't be opening the hold's doors until we gave them the thumbs-up sign on the camera.

We would then be taken two or three at a time, through a door to be processed. Anyone bitten would have a choice of getting shot or swimming back to shore.

Since they had survived this long, it wasn't my doing to question their policy.

Holding Jenny's hand, I told them both that the most important thing to me was that they survived. Whatever happened, neither of them should sacrifice themselves for me. Jenny took convincing, but she finally promised me to save herself.

They were on the way. The ship started began to pick up

speed. I kissed Jenny. "I love you, but don't wait. If something happens, you make the fucking boat."

She pushed her lower lip out and punched me in the chest, "Stop fucking cussing around the baby." We kissed and hugged. I shook Richard's hand and gave him a hug.

"Good Luck."

I don't know if I knew that I wouldn't make the ship, or that something would happen. I just knew that I was going to do whatever it took to make sure they made it.

I put the truck into gear. I noticed a few other vehicles doing the same, moving towards the pier. We were all driving as fast as possible, but we weren't cutting each other off. *Hope for humanity,* I thought.

The people in the first car got the gate open and quickly waved the next two cars through. They hopped back in his car, leaving the gate open and several of us went through. The last car stopped and the driver closed the gate.

That was also part of our directives. It might slow them down a little.

The captain had been right. They were coming out of the sand, and from under the dock, noses in the air smelling for us. We drove as close as we could parking the vehicles. I left the keys in the truck, just in case it was one of the others that came back and not me.

We ran. Backpacks over our shoulders, Jenny with her lever action, and Richard with one of his father's semi-automatics.

I had the pump shotgun and took point as we ran. There were others ahead of us, and Richard yelled, "Watch your shots!" which was excellent advice.

The first group made it to the end of the pier as the ship stopped. The door to the hold opened and a small bridge extended onto the pier. Two sailors guarded either side with some type of M-16 or AR. We'd been told they would only shoot if something not human was trying to board the ship.

The captain had been very specific. "We don't have enough

ammunition to protect you before you board and we will not waste any, if you cannot fight your way on board."

Fight our way was what we did. A large man, his family in tow, carried a baseball bat and had taken up a position on the dock to guard the bridge. The bat made quick work of several zombies that had climbed from the sea as his family boarded. Jenny and Richard were almost at the bridge when both the sailors fired. I saw two zombies fall back into the water.

I shot another, pumped in another round, and shot another. Jenny and Richard jumped into the hold. I turned and stood guard with the man with the baseball bat.

"I'm Nick," I said.

"Gary, that's my family. The others yours?" He grunted the last bit as he swung the bat to take out another one.

My shotgun was empty. I pulled out my golf club and drove it into the skull of another as I placed my boot on its chest and kicked.

I felt it then, one of its hands was raking down my leg. I didn't know if that made me contagious, but I was sure the ship would not take me on at this port.

"Give me the bat and get on board," I told Gary. "I'm not bit, just a scratch, but I'm sure the captain won't let me on board like this. I'll hold them off as long as I can." He tossed me the bat. "Tell my family I love them and if I don't turn in the next few weeks, I'll catch the next ship." As I smacked my first zombie in the head with a baseball bat, I thought, *Damn, that feels good.* I yelled, "Make it sound better than that, okay."

He shouted back over his shoulder, "You got it."

I heard Jenny scream and saw Gary restrain her. I kept fighting. When the ship moved back from the dock, I started walking. I fought my way back to shore. I had gone to a few batting cages over the years, but I'd never encountered anything like this. When I got to the parking lot, my arms were about to fall off. I threw the bat in the back of the truck and jumped in. I reached the gate quickly and thought of ramming it. But I didn't want to fuck it up for the next group of stragglers. Besides, I could be dying anyway. I quickly got out. Keeping my head on a swivel, I managed to open the gate and made it through. I didn't see any humans that hadn't made the boat. *One for the good guys!*

I was tired, but not in too bad a shape all things considered. I drove for a bit, found a place to rest up, and cleaned my wound. All in all, it wasn't a bad scratch. It might not even have been their claws or fingernails. Perhaps I'd just hurt myself on a board. I used the siphon to fill up the tanks and headed back to Don's.

Why Don's? Well, I figured that if I could make it there, I could perhaps talk to the ship and let Jenny know I was okay. I'd find out from the captain how long he wanted me to wait before I would be able to join them. He would know more about this than anyone.

Don wasn't happy to see me. It took me a long time standing outside his gate to convince him that I wasn't a zombie that could talk.

"If I was a scum-sucking zombie, I wouldn't tell you that," he finally said, and we agreed that I wouldn't bring in any weapons. If I started to Z out, he could shoot me and I wouldn't hold it against him.

We reached out to the ship, and for a few tense minutes I worried that it had been a trap, or a setup or something, but the captain said, "They are on board. All is well. No one is infected." He paused and added, "Gary says, please bring his bat with you. He said that he used that to hit the home run in his senior year and win the game for the Wildcats." We both laughed. He kept his mic open while he did so. I liked him. He had already consulted with different doctors on board. If I could make it until their next run in four weeks, I would join them.

"The baby. He is fine," was the first thing that Jenny said.

"They can tell this early?" I asked stupidly. Pam and I weren't able to have kids and now, somehow a miracle was underway. Don looked at me with the same look I had on my face. I hadn't told him that she was pregnant.

"No silly. I just know. He's going to be a strong man like his father. So hurry up and meet us. I talked to the doctors and if you survive the scratch, they may be able to help. One of the doctors on the ship knows a lot about alternative medicine. There is hope. Stay alive for me."

I couldn't hold back the tears. I didn't care if Don saw me. *Hopefully he does not think that is a sign of being a zombie... tears.*

I told them that I would be there in four weeks. Then I looked at Don and asked, "Can I eat your brains?" And we both laughed, thinking of an old zombie movie we had both seen, yelling "brains" at the same time.

I used alcohol on the inside and outside of the wound. I didn't see any of the black lines that would have indicated an infection.

I didn't want to be a risk to Don, so I headed home. I told him that I would check in a few days and there was something I wanted his help with. He'd already guessed what I wanted and nodded in agreement.

I wasn't sure why, but for the first time in a long time I thought that things might work out.

AFTERWARD

Two days after I'd left Don, I got sick as a dog. I wasn't sure if I was coming down from the stress of the last weeks, whether my original sickness was kicking in, or whether the scratch was beginning to turn me into one of them. I had a high fever and I cleaned out what was left of my medicine cabinet.

I waited until I felt normal again before visiting Don. *All I needed to do was sneeze and he'd shoot me.*

I kept an eye on the scratches and they healed as good as any scratches ever did. They stopped bleeding and by the end of the following week the scabs had fallen off. Either I had beat it, or I'd never had it.

When I got back to Don's, he asked, "Any desire for brains, or any other parts of my flesh?"

We laughed, shook hands, and hugged.

"Thanks for doing this," I said to him. He had talked to the boat a few more times. He'd told them that they'd just missed me, but that I was at home. It was nice of him to keep their hope alive.

The captain said everything was fine and Jenny said that Gary and his family had adopted them. He handed me a newspaper. The Royal Examiner, he had it turned to the sports section. The headline ran, 'Grand Slam home run for Gary…' The article named the other kids who were on the bases and mentioned that "Athey scored first…", and then continued about how proud the coach was of the team.

"When I heard his story, I thought I had that paper. Took me a little searching but I found it. I'll put it in an envelope for his family." Smiling, I took it.

"You would come with me?"

He shook his head. "You go, and if you find yourself on some wonderful island, have yourself a Mai Tai for me."

That was the end of the discussion. Don didn't like to leave his house even if the world ended. I handed him an inventory of all I had in my place that might be useful to him later on.

He climbed into my new truck. I had gone to one of the dealerships on 522 and picked out another one. The old one was good but once you hit 55, it started to shake. That's why I got a new one.

We didn't spend much time outside. We just hopped in the truck and headed out. I still thought they could detect any smell way too easily.

In my mind, I saw you smelling the air and wondered if you knew who I was.

Don and I got here this morning. It took us a while to clear out some that were walking about in the cemetery, coming out of their graves. Don stood on the back of the truck and shot them while I drove around. Then he stood guard while I broke the lock to the shed that held the backhoe.

I felt odd digging up your grave. I remember throwing a rose on your coffin after they'd lowered you in. I think that I saw it when I got down to the vault, but that could have been my imagination.

I've never done anything like this, but it was something I had to do. The thought of you down there clawing your way out of that concrete crypt for all eternity was too much to take.

Now here I was. Don and I had talked about what I would do. He stayed in the truck. He would beep the horn if he saw any others.

I am sorry about the net but it was the only way I could think of to not have you bite me.

I am not sure what I should do. Are you even in there, Pam? Can you hear me? I should have just dropped some dynamite in there. Don must have had some stashed in his living room.

I wanted you to know that I was going to find Jenny and Richard. I am not Richard's father, but I'll do my best to protect him. I did talk to the ship's doctors and told them what was wrong with me. They told me they thought they could help. I can't believe it. I might live after all.

You would like Jenny, you really would. She is good for me. She reminds me a lot of you. I know, I know, you don't want to hear that and I'm sorry. I do love you.

Did you just gnash your teeth harder when I said her name? That had to be my imagination.

If only I could give you a hug, to wrap my arms around you one last time. To kiss you the way I didn't get a chance to kiss you before you passed. I had asked Don to bring me here in the event that I turned at his place, so you and I would be able to walk hand in hand for all eternity.

Yes… yes, I know. It's a pipedream. Don would have shot me if I'd sneezed. There was no way he'd would driven a zombie asking him for a ride to your grave.

I am sorry, my love, I must go. Fuck, it is odd standing here looking down at you. I can see that you want me to slip and fall. Wouldn't that just suck?

What was that? Shit. Don is either impatient or I need to go. I love you.

Thank you my sweet, wonderful Pam. You came into my life

AFTERWARD

at the perfect time, and I was mad at you when you left. Fuck, I'm crying.

DAMN IT, DON, STOP WITH THE HORN!

I wish I had the strength to do what I should. I should put you out of your misery, and make it quick and painless. I know what I'm risking by letting you out of your grave, but I don't care. The world is yours now Pam, my darling.

I have to go. I take some solace in knowing that you'll hear my voice on the solar-powered tape player I've placed around your neck. I wonder whether I knew I would be back here when I started recording. You look so beautiful in your wedding dress. I remember how the mortuary thought I was crazy for burying you in it, but now my bride, you are free.

Goodbye my love.

I'm going to find Jenny. I will try to live.

The End

FROM THE AUTHOR

 This my fourth novella, and my first Zombie story. I hope that you enjoyed the ride.

I don't know what my next story will be about, but I promise I'll do my best to make it entertaining.

To learn more about David Musser and discover more Next Chapter authors, visit our website at www.nextchapter.pub.

MUSIC PLAYLIST

I find that music helps me focus when I write. I hope you'll enjoy my playlist.

Patches – Clarence Carter
Magic – The Cars
Pretty Fly (For a White Guy) – The Offspring
Smooth – Santana
Beth – Kiss
Kiss – Prince
Somebody That I Used to Love – Gotye
Our House – Madness
One Night in Bangkok – Murray Head
Ghosts – Sugarhouse
Loser – Beck
Ain't No Rest for the Wicked – Cage the Elephant